HEAT 16

HEAT 16

DAVID PAUL MILLER

Mystery and Suspense Press
New York Lincoln Shanghai

HEAT 16

Mystery and Suspense Press
an imprint of iUniverse, Inc.

For information address:
iUniverse, Inc.
2021 Pine Lake Road, Suite 100
Lincoln, NE 68512
www.iuniverse.com

ISBN: 0-595-27424-2 (pbk)
ISBN: 0-595-74641-1 (cloth)

Printed in the United States of America

1

Karl "Carly" Nichols saw the sign on top of St. Basil the Great High School's athletic field blink *PLAY BALL.* His stomach ached. The pain felt subdued because he'd be dressing in his uniform No. 38 as varsity fullback for the first game. It was like his feelings for girls: taut-edged nerves.

Coach Tuttle used him like a hammer against the opposition, Edwardsville High School's 'Shires. Its star line backer, Buck McKoy, concentrated on Carly. Whether off left or right tackle, McKoy ran over to get him.

When it started to storm, the air became thick. The turf slipped and slopped. McKoy kept up his hard tackles, ripping Carly's jersey, pushing him into mud. On the last play of the game, McKoy kneed him in the stomach.

He cried out, collapsing curled up. His stomach felt like it was shot. His brain reeled. He tried to tear off his jersey and rip away the agony. His teammates stood over him, helpless, until Coach Tuttle muscled through the uniforms.

Carly looked up. He saw the coach reach for his shoulder.

"Where do you hurt, son?"

"The belly."

Tuttle stuck a tube of smelling salts under Carly's nose. The stark smell stung like a hornet, but it worked.

"That's better," Carly said.

His teammates carried him, arms wrapped around, off the field into the dressing room. He sat, arms over his stomach, writhing, on a bullpen bench. Teammates crowded around. The coach came up.

"All right," Tuttle said, checking Carly's status. "Listen up. Give him some air. We beat the Hogs. Carly helped a lot."

Tuttle's acknowledgement of his value to the team gave him a tremendous lift. He'd learned to accept every injury as a given, but he was grateful for being singled out after his fall. Teammates backed away. He started to undress slowly.

The others slammed on the showers, tore off their muddy jerseys, cleats, and pants and dropped them in bins. Steam filled the concrete block bullpen. Exhaust fans pulled air outside. The floor squished with grime and washed-up suds.

He stood under the showerhead and sighed. The hot water pelted his sore muscles. When he bent over to start scrubbing his legs, a stabbing pain stopped him. He gasped and stood perfectly still, waiting for the pain to subside. When it throbbed like a compressor, he knew something was terribly wrong.

Dressed, he asked Jack Mitchem to give him a ride home.

Mitchem was a muscle-bound 16-year-old. His face was horribly pimpled, and he needed a friend. He drove an expensive SUV with a logo on the driver's door. A rival in many ways, like golf and with girls, his competitiveness was gorged with a bent toward thrills and dares. He lived on the eastern edge of town in a fine home, while Carly lived on the western part. Mitchem had to go out of his way to take Carly home.

"You know you owe me for this?" Mitchem said when they climbed into the SUV.

"Definitely going to crimp my style," Carly said, his arms folded over his belly.

"I always feel at least a little better after washing up and changing clothes."

"Not me. It feels like a red-hot ember."

Mitchem reached to tickle Carly's stomach. Carly cringed and jerked away.

"It's not funny, Jack. Just get me home."

At 6:00 P.M. the next day, Carly's older brother, Mark, came home from work for dinner. He was a dry cleaner delivery person after school. When basketball season began in a few weeks, Mark would leave work and start varsity center because of his tremendous height. He drove the Clean'Um Cleaners truck up the driveway outside Carly's window and went inside the four room house.

Carly heard him talking with Mom and Dad in the living room a few feet from his bedroom doorway. Mark came into the bedroom, looking concerned.

"Spent the whole day in bed, did ya?" he said.

"That's an understatement."

"I'm taking you to the ER."

Mom and Dad were at the bedroom doorway, looking grave. Mom took a 103 temperature in Carly's ear.

St. Francis' Hospital was in the center of town. Dad Nichols had worked on its construction as a laborer for the Pieper Building Company just as he had with St. Basil the Great High School.

Carly doubled over from pain when he walked into the ER. Mom, Dad, and Mark waited inside a curtained cubicle while Doctor Szezy, the sports doctor for St. Basil's teams, examined Carly's stomach by pressing down.

Carly's yell carried far beyond the ring of curtains. Doctor Szezy blanched and ordered a blood test. Carly's temperature was a hundred four. After swift results, orderlies moved Carly to a hospital room. Szezy came in. He was gentler with his examination this time, merely touching the skin, not pressing. He stumbled when he spoke giving the news.

"Your folks gave permission, and I've called in a surgeon. I'm afraid you have appendicitis."

Two males nurses came in and carefully shaved the hair off his belly while his parents and brothers waited outside.

2

Orderlies lifted Carly off his bed into a cart. They took him upstairs in a huge elevator to the operating room. An anesthetist gave him a shot in the arm and made him count down from a hundred. He pretended to count upward on the 14 Stations of the Cross of Jesus, and he made it to the ninth, or 91 on the doctor's descending scale. He drifted off to sleep, feeling good.

He saw dots before his eyes. The dots materialized into a person. Amazed, he drew a deep breath. It was a beautiful girl dressed in white scrubs. She compressed her hands against his chest, reached in and pulled out one of his ribs. He let out a blood-curdling yell and grabbed his rib back.

When he woke up from the operation, he felt his chest. All his ribs were intact and in place. He had dreamed the whole thing, down to the blood-curdling scream.

He saw himself full of tubes. They were intravenous lines connected to his arms. A long yellowish drain came out of his belly and was clipped over the side of his bed. It flowed into an ugly looking pouch. He groaned.

The dour Doctor Szezy played with the drain, which made Carly cringe. Szezy prohibited visitors for 48 hours, except for Mom.

She slept in an artificial leather hospital chair next to Carly's bed and made-do with a blanket and her rosary beads.

"We almost lost you," she said. "Your heart stopped and they had to work hard to bring you back. Your appendix burst."

"What day is it?"

"Monday after the game. August thirtieth, nineteen ninety-nine. Clinton is still the President."

She tried to entertain him with reminiscences aloud about her Nichols' boys in sports. When they were all in middle school and Tuttle was its coach, Tuttle had driven Mark, Carly and Eddie to Chicago for a Cub's game, a Bear's game and a Bull's game.

"Tuttle was recruiting you without saying as much," she said. "Do you remember those days?"

Carly nodded weakly.

He felt totally out of the spectrum of sports. His body was beaten him down to a knot, a mere lump on the planet. He had to be something more than a bump.

He thought of the lovely soft skin of Pudge Roos in his arms. He had hope. But he had to control himself.

Mom, Dad, Father Joe, and Sister Virginia in journalism class had made their case for abstinence as clear as the Bells of St. Mary's. Impurities with Pudge Roos could be confessed anonymously to Father Joe. He'd resolved to avoid her in the future, but that was not as clear as a bell.

He switched girlfriends to avoid the occasion of sin. His told Mark he wanted to date Mary Lou Reiley.

The next day, Father Joe, his pastor at St. Andrew's Church, administered the sacrament of the anointing of the sick. Carly noticed Father's bushy eyebrows and thick lips when the holy oil went from his thumb to Carly's forehead, eyes, and lips.

His temperature immediately started to drop. Doctor Szezy put him on a menu of solid food the next day.

Mom gave him a copy of the *Chronicle's* story about his game injury. Under a byline, Mary Lou Reiley had reported that he was expected to be out for the season. He'd broken a record for yards gained by a fullback in one game at the ten-year-old high consolidated high school.

His best hope for a date with Mary Lou, despite his bad experience with her next door neighbor Pudge Roos, would be if she interviewed him as a stricken star.

He could see visitors other than this family. Sister Virginia, his journalism teacher, tried to give him a chocolate when she came to visit. It went down like a lug nut.

Jack Mitchem, his junior classmate and crosstown rival, visited. Mitchem had lost the summer junior golf championship to Carly. At the end of tournament, instead of shaking Carly's hand according to the custom of the game, Mitchem had slapped his own hands together in disappointment.

"I'm sorry I acted the way I did at the tournament."

Mitchem offered to shake Carly's hand.

Mitchem was like that. He resented driving Carly home. Now he apologized for the long-forgotten breach of golf etiquette. He had some order in his life wrong.

"You're one strong guy," Mitchem said when he shook Carly's hand. Mitchem's hand felt moist like paste.

"Not anymore," Carly said, as if to concede next year's golf tournament. He felt worse and retched Sister Virginia's chocolate in Mitchem's direction.

When more days passed since the night of the emergency operation, Doctor Szezy came in for a discharge decision.

"Your temperature is normal," he said.

He held the drain from Carly's stomach in his hand and gradually pulled it out of the flesh.

Carly felt the tube traveling under his skin like a snake slithering.

"You have a lot of internal scarring," Szezy said. He took off the bandage over the incision.

The external surface of Carly's belly looked blistered with black staples. Doctor Szezy spread white powder on the wound. The powder turned dark from the dampness soaking up the seepage from the incision. The doctor dabbed it with a puff of cotton while he looked straight into Carly's eyes. He didn't cringe this time.

"You can go home," Szezy said.

During his internment at St. Francis,' cards and letters from teammates, classmates and parishioners piled high on the sideboard dresser. Mark came in before school at 7:30 A.M. the morning of discharge.

"I served Mass for you," Mark said.

"What about the other things I'm used to doing?" Carly asked. He often did a lot more than light candles, ring bells, and bring Father Joe the wafers. He turned the lights on-and-off, swept the floor and filled the holy water dispensers.

"I skipped those," Mark said, reaching for Carly's get-well cards. He read every card. That included a flowery one, requesting an interview, by Mary Lou Reiley.

"Didn't you say you're dropping Pudge for Mary Lou?" Mark said.

"She hasn't been in for the interview."

"Are you going to ask her to the Fall ball? I'm taking Melody Malone." Mark smiled.

Melody had placed in last year's National Catholic Essay contest, with an article about her personal struggle with purity. She was also a gorgeous blonde. Mark knew how to pick 'em.

His brother's sexuality was always a matter of interest. Mark had reached puberty first. He'd talked of his purient curiosity over girls first. He was the first one disciplined by Mom and Dad for staying out late with a date. He was the first to brag about kissing, getting naked and petting a girl. He was the first one to lose his virginity in the back seat of a car (the name of the girl was still a secret).

Mary Lou visited just prior to his discharge. She wore an open cardigan sweater and the school uniform. She'd had to take a humanitarian pass to get out of class.

He'd finished dressing by dropping his pro-life cross over his bushy head. She wore one over the bosom of her sweater. She sat in Mom's vacant chair while Mom was on a break.

"Is it all right to interview you?" she asked. "I heard you weren't going to make it."

"Father Joe anointed me."

"Did you think you were going to die?" She had the bright look of anticipation. That was funny.

"Not really. But I prayed a lot, and I had a dream."

"Not an out-of-body experience, I hope."

"What's that?"

"Like you actually died but didn't. They call it 'near death' and people have these weird stories."

"No, nothing like that." He swallowed hard. "I saw a pretty lady in white scrubs. She ripped out one of my ribs. I grabbed it and put it back. Turns out the doctor had to revive my heart during the operation."

"That's fabulous. Eve came from Adam's you-know-what."

He smiled. She looked like she was ready to take Eve's job in getting at his ribs. He was glad he mentioned it. The rib thing seemed to connect him to her wavelength. She looked receptive to his asking her for a date to the Fall Ball.

Pudge Roos and she were not only neighbors but also best friends. Did she know about his date when Pudge and he got naked?

"I read your story about the game," he said, beginning his tactical approach.

"I'm not much good as a reporter." She looked down. It was like a confession without the prayers. "Dad got me the job because he thinks I want to be a writer. But it's very awkward for me. For instance, I can't go in the boys' team locker room for an interview. I have to wait outside or the boys go crazy. And my boss, Ed Newsom, drinks, plus. It just isn't worth it to me. I'm revolted."

"Wow. What about the girls' teams?"

"I can do them all right, but then there's Ed."

"I could help you get off the hook. I would take your place in a minute. It wouldn't bother me to go in the girls' locker room for interviews."

Startled, she looked at him. She was surprised he wanted in on the girls' locker room. She couldn't know about him and Pudge getting naked.

"Tell you what, Carly, you can have the job."

Her eyes twinkled as if she saw a way out of her problems. She offered something real. He saw an attraction in the power of the press. His favorite class was journalism. It could be the best break he'd ever had.

"Sure. It just isn't working out for me."

She called Newsom on Carly's hospital phone. She didn't seem either nervous or scared to call her boss. It was as though she got the job because of her powerful father, and she could drop it just as easily. Dad Reiley was the town's biggest booster for teams at St. Basil's.

"Mr. Newsom," she said resolutely, "this is Lou Reiley." She paused and took a deep breath. "I think I'm going to quit as the school's correspondent." She paused again, as if waiting for a negative response. "I found someone to take my place. Carly Nichols no less."

She quickly gave him the receiver.

Newsom told him, if he could clear it with Coach Tuttle, to show up at the *Chronicle's* office. When he relayed that to Mary Lou, she sprang out of her chair and into his arms.

3

Coach Tuttle came in the doorway while Mary Lou kissed Carly.

"Ho!" Tuttle said, quickly backing out the door.

Carly wiped his mouth from the delicious kiss.

He stood by the hospital bed. Mary Lou backed away with the intrusion just as Tuttle backed out the door. She was alone again with Carly.

"You taste salty," she said, smiling. "Like a man."

"I'd like to take you to the Fall Ball."

Tuttle showed up again at the doorway. He knocked this time.

Carly took Mary Lou's hand and led her past the leather chair to the side by the window curtain of his hospital room. His business wasn't finished, waiting for her to answer his question. He felt a gentle squeeze from her soft fingers.

"Of course I'll go with you," she said. "How would you like a ride to the paper when you sign up for the job?"

"Great."

She recognized he might have trouble driving a car for the time being. Or was she making sure he turned up to honor his commitment?

"Excuse me, Coach," she said, leaving Carly. She passed Tuttle on the way out.

She left Carly to explain his new opportunity to his old coach.

"What was that all about?"

"She resigned as the sports correspondent. They've offered me the job."

Tuttle frowned. He went farther into the room, next to Carly by the window, and sat in the soft leather chair.

"The doctor's down the hallway. I think he'll be here in a minute. We have to talk," he said.

He was an athletic 40-year-old, with specks of white hair in his sideburns, thick lips, bushy eyebrows and furrows in his forehead. He wore a department store sports coat. He was Father Joe's twin brother.

"It's a fact that you broke the record for a junior fullback," he said. "Then this fucking thing had to happen. Now you want to drop sports for writing about the teams?"

Carly cleared his throat. His loss to the team made Tuttle swear. Tuttle also exhaled like he was upset.

"Can I have your written permission to go with being the reporter or not?"

"Sure, sure," Tuttle said. He took a spiral notebook from the inside pocket of his coat and scribbled some words on a page. He ripped the note off the spiral and handed it to Carly. "But it's just until basketball season starts."

Doctor Szezy walked into the hospital room accompanied by Mom Nichols and stood by Tuttle.

The doctor described the extent and depth of Carly's recovery and rehabilitation. He had to exercise, watch his diet and take prescriptions for the pain associated with the internal scarring which continued to build up. And he had to stay home from school for a week.

"When can he play again?" Tuttle asked.

"Maybe indoors at some later time, provided he follows the regimen," Szezy said.

Tuttle looked grim.

Mom Nichols went over to Carly and held his hand. She felt dry but supremely warm. While she stood next to him, he noticed how small and frail she was. He'd grown into a great big fullback, over six feet tall. Still, they looked like mother and son in the face. She had high cheeks, a turned up nose and dark eyebrows. They both had gray eyes, supple lips and V chins.

He put his arm over her delicate shoulders and showed her Coach Tuttle's permission to write sports for *The Daily Chronicle*.

"I can get a car with the money I make," he said.

His recuperation at home started immediately. He had an appointment to have the staples removed in a week. The surface of his belly itched from the festering wound. He tore off the bandage, even if there was a little bleeding. Air assisted in the healing process, promoting scabs. He did floor exercises as part of the regimen, but carefully at first.

He slept in a bedroom with his two brothers. Eddie had the bunk bed over his, and Mark was across the 10 X 15 room in his own bed, which had a headlamp to read.

When Mark was in school, Carly used that bed and lamp to keep up with his studies. Things seemed different when he got home from the hospital. He'd had a brush with death. It made him turn inward.

He had aspirations. He wanted to be a professional man. The classic callings were law, medicine, clergy and the military. He'd seen the ads on TV for trade school and junior college. They offered many more opportunities. He knew what he wanted to be—a good boy, hard working like his dad and concerned like his mom. But he didn't know what he wanted to do with his life.

In the daily paper he read Mary Lou Reiley's final stories about the St. Basil boys' and girls' teams. On Tuesday she had a preliminary report about the upcoming games. On Friday she had a game reports with a byline.

He hovered over her words, her sentence structure and her analyses. The emphasis was on action and personalities, like her short and sweet interview about him. He knew he could do it, and the pay was a big plus.

The Church had input on what he wanted to be. His favorite saint was St. Francis. He'd read a biography of St. Francis' mortification. The man had prayed so much that scum formed on his kneecaps. Fasting had reduced him to skin and bones.

Desire was Carly's problem. It was always on his mind. He knew the rules from Dad.

To help cope, he observed the habits and views of his older brother. Mark read a lot. He worked a lot. He studied a lot. When he talked about girls, it was always in a guarded context. He didn't want to get married early like Mom and Dad.

They'd hitched almost right out of the high school at age eighteen. They were both thirty-six. Dad had worked his whole life as a laborer for the Pieper Building Company. He wasn't even a foreman, but he went every day, except for layoffs, and made enough money to support the family with Mom's supplemental income from her house parties.

Dad was a good man, a Christian, and willing to make the sacrifice. He loved Mom, never hit her, rarely swore, and he seemed to like the life he had. He kept any financial problems to himself, but Carly knew Dad made sacrifices.

He had a small beer-making machine in the basement of the house next to where Carly stored his golf clubs. It brewed a sour concoction, which Dad consumed rather than spend the money to purchase beer in bottles or cans. He was always making sacrifices like that and never complaining.

Following his boys made his day. He wanted the boys to be happy and successful "practical Catholics" like the Knights of Columbus magazine, *Columbia*, touted. He kept a not-so-secret celebratory bottle of Irish whiskey and a flask in the front closet, upper shelf, in the rear.

In a week Mom took Carly to the doctor's office, time to get permission to return to school. He was anxious to start his job as student reporter.

In his office, Szezy, the team sports' doctor, substituted for the surgeon in removing the stitches. It was a slow, meticulous job. He plucked each one with a physician's staple remover and dropped them on a paper towel.

Carly breathed hard and fast to subdue the pain. He counted more than twenty. Szezy tried to distract his attention from the jerks and jabs.

"I hear you've got a new job."

"Sports reporting, but I haven't signed up officially yet."

"I approve of that activity. I'm afraid sports participation is out for the time being."

"How long?"

"I'd be optimistic to say you can play basketball this year."

"I'm working as hard as I can."

"You have to get back some of that muscle tone, put on a little weight, 20 pounds at least."

"I feel pretty good."

"Try to get out and around, but walk. You shouldn't drive for a while. It wouldn't hurt you to work around your house, help Mom out, like sweeping the floor, washing the dishes, doing the laundry."

"I can do that."

"Do you have a girlfriend?"

"Mary Lou Reiley."

Szezy looked to one side. "Dennis Reiley's daughter?"

"Why, have you heard something about her?"

"Bright girl."

Carly smiled. "Pretty, too."

"That's the spirit, my boy." He patted Carly on the shoulder. He finished plucking the staples. "Keep up the good work."

He dabbed the wound with gauze, which reflected moisture from discharge. He dropped the gauze on the paper towel, folded the bunch of bent staples and dropped the towel in a medical wastebasket marked *disposable items*.

"We'll put your status on hold for another month. Make an appointment."

Carly went meekly to Mom, who was waiting in the reception room. He told her about helping at the house. After making the next appointment, they left for home. He offered to assist with her latest house party preparations.

She wanted him to do the laundry.

4

Carly waited outside on the stoop for Mary Lou to pick him up for the interview with Ed Newsom. He was excited at the prospects both for himself as a reporter and for her in his future. He didn't care if she wasn't punctual because she was more interesting than Pudge Roos. It gave him time to speculate about her rich family and what it could do for him.

She drove up in her folks' SUV. She wore a sweater with the school colors, gold and purple, over her uniform. She said she'd taken off with a humanitarian permission slip signed by Father Alexander, the principal. That was why she was late.

She'd put on perfume. He was pleased when she let him kiss her after he climbed in the Jeep Cherokee. Her bright blue eyes sparkled over her rosy, lightly freckled cheeks.

Was she a fetching Irish virgin or not?

The Daily Chronicle's granite-faced office building was located partway up the bluff on Eighth Street and Ninth Avenue in downtown Landers' Landing. It was two stories tall with a clear view of the Mississippi River to the east. Mary Lou parked in front, under a restricted parking sign, on the wrong side of the street.

"Aren't you coming up?" Carly asked.

"And face that drunk?"

"But you got me the job."

She shook her head. "You got you the job, remember? You talked with him on the phone. You have to go in by yourself."

He leaned over and kissed her on the cheek. He opened the door, stepped out, walked around the SUV and turned back to look at her. She leaned over the driver's side open window and settled her chin on folded arms. He thought she looked like a Siamese cat, playful and loveable.

He went inside *The Daily Chronicle's* front doorway and asked a receptionist for the location of the editorial offices. A smiling young woman in a gingham dress pointed toward a stairway on the north side of the lobby. He walked there slowly but tried to dash up the steps two at a time. He cramped along the way until he stopped dead in his tracks at the top.

He looked around at an open bullpen with a dozen desks. Each had an unoccupied computer, except for Newsom's at a far corner. He smelled the odor of newsprint. He heard the whirl and hum of the press running downstairs. The raw excitement of journalistic production crashed into his head. He walked up to Newsom, who wore a Cub's cap.

Newsom had a liver-spotted complexion and reddish cheeks, and he grinned when he looked over Carly.

"I'm not sure you pass the physical to be a reporter." Newsom had a garish sense of humor.

"Coach gave permission," Carly said, digging out from his pocket Tuttle's spiral-edged note.

Newsom took it, read it and opened a desk drawer, dropping the paper inside. Carly saw a half-pint bottle nesting under sticky notes. Newsom rummaged around and eventually drew out three pamphlets.

"Here's your style book, a list of football rules and a scoring pad," he said. "You have to drop the preliminaries in the slot at the bottom of the steps by ten on Monday night. Game stories have to be in by eleven the night of the event. We usually rewrite those to match the headline." He filled in a blank press card for the package.

Carly took the pamphlets and card and thanked him.

"Everything's not hard copy," Newsom said. "Have you got a computer?"

"I have access."

Newsom fished around in his drawer again, lifting out a key. He shut the drawer.

"That's for the door at the bottom of the steps. If someone's around when you come, ask to use a computer. There's always one available. Use Word and put your story on a disk in an envelope on my desk."

"I can do that," Carly said. "But can I use a typewriter sometimes?"

"Sure. What's important is to meet the deadlines. Either way, you should be getting up to speed about the time you have to stop."

"What if I don't want to leave?"

"When the basketball season begins, Tuttle wants you back."

"Yes, he told me. But the doctor hasn't said exactly when I can play."

"We'll see. You haven't even written your first story, yet." He turned his back on Carly, finished with instructions, and shuffled through papers laid out over his credenza.

Carly was shut out for the time being. When he backed up to leave, he looked around the bullpen. Newsom could have introduced him to others in the place, such as the editor-in-chief or the publisher, Max Able. His office was behind a door marked *private* and next to another signed *CPA*.

Without a handshake from his new boss, Carly went down the long flight of steps to the first floor landing. It faced the outside door that had the brass mail slot for his stories.

Was Newsom going to be a problem? Outside, Carly felt relieved.

Mary Lou was still parked in the restricted zone with the Jeep motor running. "Let's get something to drink," she said after he climbed in.

Her fetching voice was appealing. He wanted to talk with her about strategies for writing the preliminary story on the next game. But even if she didn't want to talk, she was more satisfactory than Pudge Roos. She was prettier and unselfish.

They pulled into the The Big Ober Root Beer Drive-in for a drink at the outside picnic table. Everyone else was in school. Maxine Oberhaus, the owner, looked at Carly suspiciously. She opened the screen and pushed out a menu. He asked for two large cups and gave Maxine five dollars. Maxine took back her menu, drew the root beer from a tank and made change.

Carly limped to the picnic table carrying the cups. Maxine came out of a side door to offer to carry the drinks. By then Carly was at the picnic table. Maxine went back inside, out of his view.

Mary Lou wanted to talk.

"Even though I gave up the job, I do like writing," she said. "I'm going to run for editor-in-chief of the *Beam* when elections come up this fall."

The *Beam* was the school paper and needed someone like her to shape it. She was getting intellectually interesting.

They had journalism class together. She liked the Irish writers, and there were plenty of them with Nobel prizes. She wanted to talk with him about them, but she did the talking.

After they drank the root beer, she drove him home. The Nichols' house was on Grove Avenue. One overgrown pine obscured the picture window in front. She pulled her Cherokee up under a basketball hoop hung on the single car attached garage. He thanked her for her help.

She had to go back to school since her excuse expired at 10:00 A.M., but she kissed him on his cheek before he climbed out of the SUV. Because he'd listened to her, she said, he was a dear.

"I might walk over to your house after school tomorrow with my dog," he said.

"'Kay," she said. "How about four o'clock?"

5

Mary Lou's house was next door to Pudge Roos', a distance of probably 400 feet in an exclusive neighborhood of landscaped homes two miles across town. Jack Mitchem lived down the road.

Her dad was a director of the New York Stock Exchange listed company, Woodbine Paper Corporation. He was a lawyer and a shining Catholic gentleman. Pudge's dad was a plastic surgeon with a clinic catering to the would-be-beautiful crowd, as the blaring TV ads said. Mitchem's folks were real estate agents.

Carly got tired walking the distance across town. Itching from his incision aggravated him, but it was worth it. His dog was a longhaired black mix weighing about 20 pounds.

Mary Lou's house was an English Tudor with three stories. The most outstanding room was made of what looked like crystal bulb protruding on one side off the living room. The house had a long, winding walkway to the front door and vestibule. He passed two lawn chairs.

When he rang her doorbell, he heard her dog bark. He leashed his on a hook under the mailbox. Mary Lou came to the door quickly. She wore a denim skirt and white blouse, smiled and let him in. Her dog was a small longhaired white terrier. She stopped barking and sniffed his sneakers.

"Meet 'Whitie'," she said. "She's been fixed."

"I call mine 'Blackie'. So has he."

"Come on," she said, grabbing his hand, "I'll show you around."

He noticed her walking at home a little differently than when she came in his room at the hospital. She slithered on her hips, rolling the steps forward in a sliding rhythm.

Pudge liked to wiggle her big bottom.

Taking his hand, Mary Lou led him down a long hallway. It was decorated with a wall clock, a mail table, a hat tree and carpeted with a dark blend.

They stopped by a double door, and she pushed it open.

In a library from a top shelf where she stretched to get it, she pulled down a book. He saw that Mary Lou's body was as thin as a rail. The front edge of her

blouse popped out of her denims. He saw her bellybutton, an outie, and the surface of her abdomen, which was slightly concave, like his after the operation. The
bones of her hips bulged against her skin.

She gave him the leather bound, gold-embossed book.

"I'm going to show that to Mrs. Johnson as a suggested topic for the school
play," she said, with a little flute in her voice. "It's an English 'cozy' about an
impoverished banker who takes care of a dog that inherits a million from a
crank."

Quite a mouthful, he thought.

"What's a 'cozy'?" he said.

"It's an endearing English old manor mystery."

He loved the way she said that.

She took the book from his hand and set it on a casual table. She grabbed his
hand.

"Come on, I'll show you my dad's greenhouse."

Off the living room, that was the porch which protruded outside like a crystal
bulb. He felt moved by its contrast with his own bungalow. His bedroom could
fit into the greenhouse.

"He raises baby wild animals," she said. "They're caged now."

"Where?"

She pointed to a corner where boxed bars were attached to the wall joined
with the living room. He walked over and saw several tiny coons behind a stainless grille.

"Where's the mother?" he asked.

She followed him and leaned over to peer in.

"That's the problem. They're orphans. He has to bottle feed them."

"Sounds maternal." He looked over at Mary Lou and down toward her
blouse. He began to sweat. The air was moist. She had no bumps for her breasts.
Her blouse was flat.

"Dad's basically retired. He has the time, so it's paternal."

There was an odor from the refuse of the coons. The heat in the greenhouse,
accompanied by moisture, seemed oppressive. She led him out of the zoo into the
living room.

All around lay alumnae reports, literature and pictures of her mom's college,
Mt. Holyoke, South Hadley, Massachusetts.

"I have a little brother, Tolly, six, and a little sister, Molly, five. But they're out
with Mom at the big zoo today." She led him to the front door. "Let's let our
dogs play."

They went outside. He unleashed Blackie, and she let Whitie run. They walked toward two lawn chairs near a catalpa tree.

"I'm going to offer mine for the school play," she said.

He realized that she was involved in a fantasy about the school play to the extent that she had it worked out to put her own pet dog in front of the audience.

"But first Mrs. Johnson has to choose your play."

"I think she will, but of course I don't know for sure. She asked for suggestions."

They stopped at the green and orange-striped canvas lawn chairs. The dogs followed in gallops.

"How would you control them onstage?" he asked.

Mary Lou slid into a lawn chair. "Mine's pretty meek." The dogs momentarily growled and barked in the browning fall grass. "Is yours?"

"I suppose I'd use a leash." He slipped into the other lawn chair.

The dogs calmed down. They curled up over the grass, eyeing each other and their masters.

Pudge Roos came over, across the unfenced grass from next door, with a plastic bottle and cups for drinks.

She wore short summer pants and had a skimpy halter bulging with her generous breasts.

"I saw the dogs romping on the lawn," she said. "Can I join the fun?" She held out the cups and plastic bottle.

"How nice," Mary Lou said.

Pudge poured the drink and gave them each a small cup. When Carly tasted the drink, he knew it was spiked.

Pudge plopped on the grass with the bottle between her legs. She seemed to notice him looking between her legs.

Mary Lou turned toward Pudge's house where her mother called her.

Pudge scooped up the bottle, said she had to run and left.

Carly watched while she romped, wiggling her butt, back to her ranch-style house.

"She's my best friend," Mary Lou said.

"Did I know that?" He set down his empty cup. The dogs immediately began to smell it.

"She saved my life once ten years ago, when we were six."

Mary Lou pointed toward the pool located in the back yard of Pudge's house.

"I was taking water into my lungs, and she pulled me out of the pool." She paused thoughtfully. "We should double date for the formal. She's taking Jack Mitchem."

Carly frowned.

"Are you uncomfortable with that?" She tossed her cup at the dogs.

"No, no. I've dated Pudge before."

"I didn't know that."

"We went to the Midsummer dance downtown."

6

Carly and Ed Newsom worked together at the St. Basil's game against Gene Tunney High in the observation booth above the football field. Newsom seemed friendlier than in the *Chronicle's* editorial offices, probably because Carly's preliminary report for the game passed inspection. There was no rewrite at all.

Newsom's responsibility at the game was to call the play over the public address system. The microphone had an on-off switch. Newsom took the name of the Lord in vain half the time he switched from on to off, as if he were uncomfortable in his hard metal seat, with the job he was doing and the company he was keeping.

Carly's responsibility was to keep the official score. He noticed Newsom take nips from a half-pint bottle.

At halftime, Carly watched the cheerleaders' program. Pudge Roos demonstrated female calisthenics. During this period, Carly noticed Newsom scratch suggestively. The guy had jock itch on top of his drinking.

He saw Newsom take out a little metal tube and dose his finger, then reach back and goose himself. He had hemorrhoids, too. It was an affliction Dad Nichols suffered from.

Carly began to think differently of Newsom, at least regarding the plunges beneath the belt. He thought he'd found the real source of Mary Lou's complaints.

She said she was revolted. It looked like he was pawing for gratification with the jock itch.

Newsom was just sick with an affliction of hemorrhoids like his own dad. Both probably suffered because of alcohol, Dad with his sour homemade brew, Newsom from his sips from the half-pint.

On Monday he saw Mary Lou after last period. He went to her locker and broached the Newsom subject.

She laughed out loud, as if she didn't believe him. She accused Carly of "falling for it."

He explained about Newsom's medicinal tube for hemorrhoids.

"That's how they do it, buddy," she said.

He thought that was pretty cynical.

"You don't know anything without seeing his asshole."

"Listen, Carly. I told you I quit because he was a drunk. But he was also playing with himself. I was revolted. I can tell the difference between that and jock or hemorrhoid itch."

"I believe you. But I also believe Ed was in pain. I know the look. My dad has hemorrhoids."

"Carly, this is going no where—like *us*," she said with a punch. She walked away.

He was stunned.

He ran after her and apologized. He wanted her to know that his observation of Ed Newsom was an honest interpretation that happened to be different from hers. She stopped, turned to face him and looked totally without sympathy.

The next day at school, in the hallway outside the principal's office by the front door, Pudge Roos congratulated Carly over his game story in the *Chronicle*.

"How've you been?" she asked. She looked expectant, because of the upcoming double date to the Fall Ball.

"'Kay. How've you been?" He looked at her blouse, then down on the floor.

"I'm on a crusade," she said. "I hear Tom Mowen, the senior class president, has appointed you to run the junior-senior brunch."

That was the initial activity on Fall Ball Day. The occasion began with a Mass in the gym, continued with a brunch in the cafeteria and ended with the dance back in the gym. The juniors had to put on the brunch as a treat for the seniors. Tom Mowen had roped Carly into running the brunch.

"So?"

"Did you know the cooks put saltpeter under the food, especially the cake?" she said. She had an impish expression.

"What's saltpeter?"

"It inhibits the male sexual drive," she said. She raised her eyebrows. He could imagine what she what thinking about his hairy body.

"We can't have that," Carly said. He meant it sarcastically, but she took it differently. She was so stupid.

"I'm glad you agree. Will you go with me to see the principal, Father Alexander, to do something about it?"

It was a dare. Like her date for the dance, Jack Mitchem, she was into dares for the thrills. She had to know he was sarcastic when he replied. No one would really want to inhibit the male sex drive. The population would go out of business.

She was pretty when she had something on her mind. She wore the school uniform, slightly smaller than regular size. She bulged, and that appealed to him. But she was a bad girl. He had to stay away from her.

"'Kay." He said it very tentatively.

She grabbed his hand. They were in the hall, outside the office, and they walked in.

It was Tuesday afternoon, the time designated in the school religious week for Father Alexander to hear confessions. The office was empty of other students, and they sat down.

The office manager was Ellie Blanchard, the married sister of the Big Ober who ran the root beer stand. She was always neatly dressed. Today Ellie wore a polka-dotted frock and sat at her desk with hands folded on top. Carly looked at the clock, behind Ellie, that was connected to the bell that rang automatically during the school day. The hands read 4:15 P.M.

"Are you here for confession?" Ellie asked.

"We need to see Father," Pudge said.

"He's not doing anything but confessions until five."

"Well, would you just ask him if he'll see Carly and me for a minute, but not for confession?"

"I'm not sure I should interrupt Father when he's praying," Ellie said.

Suddenly Father's closed private office door opened. Jack Mitchem came out. He didn't look surprised to see Pudge and Carly, especially together. He passed them into the outside hall with only a little wave of his hand.

"Next," Carly heard Father say.

Ellie got up, pushed the swinging door in the counter and went to Father's doorway. She whispered a few words, turned and faced Pudge and Carly and showed them into the private office.

The more Carly thought about Pudge's investigation into the inhibiting salt-peter, the more he felt it was a bad idea to bring up the subject with the principal.

Father was kneeling at a *prie-dieu* with a confessional screen. He stood and removed the purple stole around his neck, kissed it and draped it over the screen where penitents knelt. He went around his elaborate desk and sat in his wing chair.

"What's on your mind?" he said.

Father was St. Basil the Great High School's first and only principal. As a young scholar from Ecole Sanctus D'Spirit College, he was on loan from the

Archdiocese of Chicago to the local diocesan department of education according to word around the school. He had black hair, hazel eyes and a bent angular nose that looked as if it'd been broken at one time. He looked twice as old as Carly. Even though his liturgy was interrupted, he spoke softly as if he knew the office was empty of students waiting to go to confession.

Carly and Pudge sat in hard wooden chairs in front of the chiseled hickory desk. Carly was not about to speak first, since the idea was Pudge's. The desk had a panel of crosses and sacred hearts. He concentrated on gazing at them because he felt ready for a dressing down.

"I'm here to file a complaint," Pudge said.

"About what?"

"I've heard the cooks in the cafeteria put saltpeter under the cake."

"They may use a little preservative once in a while, but I don't know anything about saltpeter. Isn't that a chemical?"

"It's a drug on young men," Pudge said.

"Oh, no. We don't use any drugs in our food."

Carly stood, embarrassed. "Thanks for your information," he said. "Come on, Pudge. I told you, you were wrong."

Pudge stood. "No, you didn't. It was your idea to see Father. You're the food chairman."

"Oh," Father said. "Are you running the brunch for the Fall Ball, Carly?"

"Yes."

"Rest assured all the food cooked by the parish mothers is as pure as the driven snow," Father said, looking at Carly.

"Thank you, Father."

Carly and Pudge turned and walked out, past Ellie listening at the door, into the hallway. Jack Mitchem stood outside, smoking, by the building's front door near the main office. Dropping his cigarette, he bolted inside and grabbed Pudge's hand. They went off down the hallway, leaving Carly standing alone.

He distinctly heard Mitchem ask Pudge if "it worked."

The whole thing had been a ruse set up by the mischievous Mitchem, who was at it again.

If Carly had any guts, he would tell Mary Lou to cut off the double date. They could probably go with Mark and Melody Malone unless their decision was set in stone.

He wondered if Mary Lou would be upset if he asked her to change the arrangements on the basis of an elaborate and extended joke about saltpeter under the cake at the junior-senior brunch. It just wasn't a good enough reason to spoil her plans. And maybe Mark and Melody wouldn't want to go with them anyway. He had to remember that Mark wasn't a virgin. Both Mark and Melody were seniors, ready to leap off into life.

7

When Carly got his first check from the *Chronicle,* he asked Mary Lou to drive him to open an account at the Landers' Landing Bank & Trust. She had access to the SUV while he still didn't have the money saved to buy a decent car. They went inside together. It was an old-fashioned bank with a vaulted ceiling, marble floor, two open and 13 closed teller grilles, staid looking loan officers and a rigid new accounts desk person.

He was turned down because of age. He had to take a signature card home for Mom to co-sign and be named on the ATM card. But he wasn't angry. It was to use proceeds from his job.

When they left with the cards, Carly saw Pudge Roos come in. Mary Lou grabbed her hand.

Pudge gave Carly a toothy grin.

"Listen to me," Mary Lou said to Pudge. "We've only days to get our dresses for the ball."

"How are you, Carly?" Pudge said, ignoring Mary Lou.

"Better." He looked down, but it did no good. Not only did she have a toothy grin, making fun of him, but bulging breasts.

"Where are you, girl?" Mary Lou said.

"We'll get together, honey," Pudge said. "I'll call."

Pudge walked past them up to a teller's window.

"What was that all about?" Mary Lou said.

"Pudge found out about the cooks using saltpeter under cake at the cafeteria, and she's on a crusade to have Father Alexander get rid of it."

"Saltpeter?"

"Yeah, it's like this substance that inhibits the male sexual drive."

"Sort of a reverse handle, huh?" Mary Lou said. "I didn't know the cafeteria was putting drugs in our cake."

"Father wouldn't allow anything like that," Carly said. But he hadn't wanted to tell Mary Lou about his suspicions for sure after seeing the principal with Pudge. They walked outside the bank.

"Have you noticed anything?" Mary Lou said.

"You mean, don't I have any more wet dreams?"

"Whatever you have, Carly."

"No, I haven't noticed anything. Do I seem different?"

"No."

She frowned.

"Well, Tom Mowen appointed me to organize the brunch. As the food chairman, I can talk with the cooks. They're from the parishes. The menu has cake on it."

"You seem to know a lot about this saltpeter stuff."

"The cooks know what they're doing. Some guys could use a dose."

"You mean Jack Mitchem? He'll be in the same car with us."

"We can always cut out if it gets yeasty. Or we could join in."

"Join in what?"

"The fun."

Mary Lou stopped in her tracks. She put her hands on her hips.

It happened just as a couple passed them on the sidewalk.

"Hey, man," the boy in the couple said, "don't you do that."

"Leave it to me," Carly said.

"Yeah, man," the boy said.

He was far enough away so Carly couldn't pop him in the mouth. But Carly gave him the finger. Mary Lou didn't.

Mary Lou and her friends, including Pudge, wore old clothes to Mass and the brunch. Carly, the chairman, wore a big white bib. He made a point to show Pudge that under the cake there was something on the plate that looked like sugar but which wasn't sweet. It could be potassium nitrate, saltpeter.

He asked Mark, who ate every bit of the cake, wetting his finger, dabbing the little white crystals of white stuff and licking them down.

"There's nothing wrong with it, man," Mark said. "Actually, I think it's sodium chloride, salt."

Pudge passed the word and much of the cake went uneaten.

The cooks from the parishes who prepared the meal were responsible. The blame didn't seem to filter down to Carly. The rest of the brunch of baked ham, potato salad, green beans, hot rolls, milk and ice cream cups went down without a hitch.

Mary Lou told Carly that her friends were going to spend the afternoon getting hair-repair and dressing for the night. She wanted him to help get her house ready for an after-dance party. Like at church, fixing a place was something he could do. But when he arrived at her house, he had a tremendous cramp in his stomach.

In the bathroom he noticed a little excretion from a corner of the long scabbing scar in his belly. It throbbed badly. He also felt aroused. He decided that when he dressed formally for the dance he'd wear an athletic cup so any arousal wasn't obvious.

He set out mints, nuts and chips for the party. He saw Mary Lou empty a bottle of vodka into a huge punch bowl in the library. He sampled it when she was in another room. The punch was so diluted that he could barely feel the effects of the liquor.

She took him to the tuxedo store to pick up his suit and left him off at his house. He was supposed to get her for the dance about 8:00 P.M., but she called at 6:00 P.M. and said she would rather pick him up in her parents' SUV. She wanted to take more people to her party afterward. She explained that she'd called her parents at their out-of-town place, Aunt Gertrude Reiley's. They'd given permission to use the family vehicle while they were gone with her dad's Cadillac.

He dressed about the same time as Mark. Mark put on the straps for an athletic cup as if he had the same problem when he danced that Carly had but'd independently arrived at the remedy. Since Mark wasn't a virgin, Carly didn't feel it was a little strange to add this touch of protection himself.

They tied each other's bows. Carly's was black. Mark's was red for his senior status. Mark was doubling with Tom Mowen and left first. Carly waited in the living room for Mary Lou, holding her flower, while his family admired his dressy outfit and pinned a carnation on his lapel.

The music for the dance wasn't live. The committee had decided to donate the difference between the cost of a live band, about $2,000, and a DJ, about two hundred. It was supposed to be in the form of a gift from the junior class, $1,800, which would then be given to KidsRight, a pro-life organization active in Landers' Landing, in the name of the senior class. Father Alexander announced over the loudspeaker that the donation earned a letter of recognition from the bishop, who'd forwarded a copy of the award to the pope.

Mary Lou, Pudge, Carly and Mitchem arrived about 8:30 P.M. Hers and Pudge's new dresses, held together with zippers and hooks, were appropriately light, almost see-through in the flurry of the arrival, Carly noticed. They were decorated with flowers.

By 9:00 P.M. Carly felt sick. Bleeding from his incision had started again, plus cramps. Mary Lou sat out several dances with him, playing with her party favors and chatting with Pudge, before Mitchem and others asked her to dance. She wore a dainty dance book on her wrist and conscientiously wrote down all the names of her suitors.

Eventually she kicked off her shoes and hopped around the floor, pogo-ing, to the DJ's requests, and came back for more. The activity never led to slam-dancing under the disarming eyes of the chaperons, Father Alexander and Coach Tuttle with his wife, Louise.

Father Alexander wore a sport coat. He told Carly, when the pogo-ing picked up, that the rhythm was amusing.

There was no rush to go home, but gradually the tables set up in the gym emptied. By 11:00 P.M. the crowd was down to 15 or 20 couples who were going to Mary Lou's. A big gang of seniors left earlier. Carly heard they had reserved rooms at the Lumber up Motel, which had a large swimming pool. They had parental chaperons for the purpose of operating as designated drivers. Carly heard that the chaperons were the folks of the class presidents. Since Tom Mowen was the senior class president and double dating with Mark and Medlody Malone, Carly guessed that his brother was at that party, but Mark hadn't mentioned it. They probably would mix with a lot of drinking, physical teasing and encounters, Carly speculated.

Jack Mitchem deserted Pudge Roos. Mary Lou heard he went with Leon Sweeney in another vehicle to go to the swimming pool. But no one saw a scene between Roos and Mitchem when they split. Pudge seemed content to go with the Reiley party, sitting in the back seat of the SUV. She stroked Carly's head once despite the fact that he sat next to Mary Lou.

At the after-dance party in Mary Lou's home, everyone headed for the big punch bowl because of word of mouth about the vodka, except Carly. He knew that the vodka thing was a ruse of dilution.

Mary Lou showed people around in the greenhouse. She actually nursed one of the coons with a bottle her dad kept in a refrigerator by the cage. That turned out to be an opportunity for Pudge to get Carly in a corner and start talking intimately. He instantly felt pressed.

"I hope you know that what I did on our last date was because I love you," she said. "When you get tired of Mary Lou I would take you back in a second."

"That's just because Mitchem ducked out on you."

She grabbed his hand and led him to the front door and out onto the lawn. Over on the grass, sheltered by a catalpa tree, he saw a couple sitting with their backs to the bark, holding hands and kissing. The feature of the catalpa was concave brown spiny seeds.

Pudge dragged Carly along toward the tree. He staggered unwillingly, looking back toward the windows where he noticed Mary Lou in the greenhouse feeding the coon.

Pudge reached the far side of the catalpa tree trunk. She wore a fragrant gardenia. She grabbed and placed one of his hands on one of her breasts and kissed him on the lips. He held steady like a pole.

"Don't you feel anything?" she whispered.

"Of course I do." It was a delicious kiss, and he puckered his lips. The gardenia smelled very sweet.

"I feel great. Here's your chance, Carly."

She moved her hand down and closed her eyes.

He remembered Pudge's lovely breasts and blossoming nipples while they played in the front seat of her car at the Midsummer dance. It was like holding treasure.

His feelings exploded. He began to sweat. The pain in his belly went away. He loved the beautiful body in front of him and put his hand on her bosom, gently squeezing. His arousal grew, but he recognized temptation and wavered. He also felt disloyal to Mary Lou.

"I'm not sure I want your souvenir, Pudge."

"What's wrong with me?"

When he didn't answer, she unhooked one side of her bodice, dropping the flimsy cloth pinned with the gardenia and exposing her breast.

He ran his finger over her growing nipple.

"You should be more modest."

She pressed against him, reaching with her hands. Suddenly, she opened her eyes.

"You've got an athletic cup."

She backed away.

"Well," she said.

"I can't take it out. It's strapped in. I'm sorry."

She hooked up her dress, picking off the gardenia and tossing it to the ground.

He felt disappointed.

"You're some onion." She was exasperated.

"Well, you try to lead me. I'm supposed to lead you."

"I'll stop if you want."

"'Kay, let's stop."

His arousal waned.

She held him around the neck, stood on her tiptoes, pulled down his head and blew in his ear.

She quickly headed across the lawn for her own house.

He grabbed the first ride home, avoiding Mary Lou, who was absorbed in the excitement of her party with the others.

8

Carly went to Mass and confession the first thing the next day, Sunday morning. Mary Lou called at noon, peeved.

"What happened to you last night?"

"Any complaints from your folks?" he asked evasively.

"They're still out of town with Tolly and Molly."

"I need to tell you something."

"As long as it's not too serious."

"It's serious. Boy, is it serious."

"Well, I think running off without kissing me good night is pretty serious."

"I apologize." He couldn't quite bring himself to tell her he'd played with Pudge. Mary Lou was preempting his thoughts. It was a bad habit of hers, anticipating what people were going to say. It masked the unopened truth about his petting Pudge. He dropped the notion of telling her over the phone. She charged ahead, accepting his apology.

"I'd like you to go with me to see Mrs. Johnson tomorrow about the play."

"All right."

"Meet me by my locker after last period, and we'll take the book to her. She'll be impressed that the play ran in London. Then we can go home and clean up before the folks get back with my little brother and sister at six. By the way, Pudge called, and she's sick. She can't help us."

Pudge sick? He should call her, but he hesitated. Connecting would only encourage her and tend to sink him further into lust.

In Mrs. Johnson's classroom the next day, Carly met Mary Lou with the gold-bound book of *The Song of the Dancing Dog* by Gustov Hammerlink.

Mabel Johnson was a graduate of a traveling ice skating troupe, the *Ice-It Show*, before marrying a local lawyer and settling into teaching and raising a family. She was famous amongst the players for her even temper and silly mouth. Her favorite word was *dearie*. She was also the part-time girls' basketball coach.

When Mary Lou told her about the London production, Mrs. Johnson said she would consider *The Song of the Dancing Dog* for the school's play. Several other students had offered their ideas, but she told Mary Lou that hers was the best one so far.

Mary Lou was thrilled. She asked Carly how his dog was doing.

"Blackie's better than his master."

"Aren't you feeling good, honey?" In the school hallway, she towed on his arm, looking up at his broad shoulders,

"I have to see Doc Szezy tomorrow for my one month follow-up since the operation. I'm worried he won't let me resume playing. Basketball preseason starts in a few more weeks. Mark's already got the play book."

"Want me to go with for moral support?"

"That would be nice." He smiled.

On the way to clean her mom's house, she drove her Mom's old station wagon, which didn't have bucket seats like the SUV. He sat beside her on the bench seat, and he got the distinct feeling of warmth from her body.

Pudge showed up anyway at the Reiley residence to help clean. She seemed to recover miraculously from her party sickness. Carly tried to avoid looking at her bouncing breasts and wiggling bottom.

When they finished sweeping, washing dishes, and straightening up the living room, library, and kitchen, they watched videos.

Pudge got the wicked idea of calling the Twister Sandwich Shop downtown, a house of ill-repute. She asked with a serious voice for a hot dog sandwich in the name of Jonathon John-John to go, and slammed down the receiver.

She was teasing Mary Lou with her inside joke from the advance at the party, and simultaneously she was tormenting Carly, with her outhouse manner for backing down after he touched her. He really hated the way she forced herself on people.

Mary Lou laughed but quickly changed the subject.

She told Pudge about the presentation of the play to Mrs. Johnson.

"What a neat idea," Pudge said. "I want to try out."

The next day he saw Mary Lou before going to the doctor. He intended to straighten himself out with her, but he never got around to broaching the subject of Pudge's encroachment. After Pudge's call to The Twister Sandwich Shop, he thought Mary Lou knew how raunchy Pudge was anyway.

It was strange how the mind made excuses for the emotions, but it was happening to him a lot lately.

On the way to the doctor's office, he cuddled up to Mary Lou on the bench seat. She didn't tell him to move back, lending support and encouragement. He said he was afraid the sports doctor would continue his ban against resuming ball play.

Mary Lou had to wait in the reception area while he went for the thorough physical, beginning with being weighed on an electronic scale and extending to fluid samples. Afterward, Carly sat in his Szezy's office to talk about the results.

The doctor's desk was a mess, piled with brown folders and medical reports. On the walls behind, the doctor displayed degrees, certificates and memberships. He also had a little plastic skeleton dangling from a metal hook off the wing of a floor lamp.

"I can see you're still pretty stiff," Szezy said.

"At the dance last Saturday I had some bleeding from the incision."

"That's just superficial. If you had a hernia, you would've felt a sharp pain."

"What's a hernia?"

"A rip in the abdominal wall, like a stitch tearing open."

Carly nodded. He had sharp pains, but they always went away. He understood what was to be avoided. But he wanted to know the answer to his most important question.

"Can I play ball starting in a month?"

He held his breath. He slid his tongue over his lips. He felt his heartbeat pick up because he knew Doctor Szezy had the power to release him or not for the varsity with Mark.

"I'm afraid not just yet," Szezy said. "You have to remember I advised a regimen. Have you been adhering to it?"

"I've been walking a lot, and doing my floor exercises. I'm eating like a wrestler."

"But you haven't gained any weight. In fact, you've lost weight. I believe we set a goal of gaining twenty pounds."

"What else can I do besides stuff myself?" Carly looked at the plastic skeleton.

"Are you worried about something?"

"Just the usual." Carly said. The doctor waited for a more complete answer. "My job as a sports reporter takes me out of town with the team, but I like that. We went to Ripper, and they're one of the worst teams to play against."

"That's way up in Wisconsin, isn't it?"

"Yeah, it's an overnight. I sat in metal folding chair by the bus driver because the team took up all the soft seats. That did bother me. But I ate the usual T-bone steak after the game at the hotel restaurant and slept pretty good afterward."

"Let's be on the safe side. Your muscle tone is poor. I don't think you've been working out like you should."

"Well, with the writing, and studies, and my girlfriend—"

"I see. I'll make a deal with you. Get that muscle tone back, and gain twenty pounds, and I'll release you."

Carly stood, towering over Doctor Szezy's desk. He extended his hand to accept the deal. Szezy shook it and smiled like his teeth were hurting.

But Carly had to make an appointment to return in another month, which was two weeks before basketball season was to begin. He went out to face Mary Lou and give her the bad news. He felt his eyes sting. He was trapped.

"I'm still benched," he said.

"I'm sorry. You can swear if it'll help."

He didn't want to violate the slogan of the Knights of Columbus against taking the name of the Lord in vain.

The next day he got a letter from sports editor Ed Newsom correcting his spelling of the word *their,* which wasn't spelled *thier.* He called Mary Lou at home. He wanted a reminder of her confidence in him.

She talked about her expectations to revamp the school paper, the St. Basil's *Beam.* Election for editor-in-chief was only a few weeks away.

The subject turned to what she wanted to be in life. She had to have an education at her mom's alumnus, Mt. Holyoke. And she said she'd rewritten a story 15 times before she intended to submit it a magazine.

"What do you want to be?" she asked. She sounded relaxed, and she made a trivial error in bunching words together. "What do you wannabe? I think you'd be a good teacher."

"I can't even spell." He told her about Newsom's spelling correction letter.

It wasn't a good move. He looked stupid for misspelling a common pronoun.

"You'd make a good *preacher* if not a good *teacher,*" she said.

She understood. She made her understanding sound like a silly rhyme.

No one had ever told him he might have a vocation, and she couldn't be serious about that. After he ravished her in bed, she'd change her mind.

"You sound like Sister Humility."

"Well, I wasn't suggesting you be a priest. I was asking about your inclination."

"I incline toward you."

"If we weren't on the phone, I kiss you for that."

"I'll blow you a kiss." He exhaled into the receiver.

She paused and giggled. "I caught it." She hung up.

9

Carly accumulated enough cash to buy an old car. He was still having trouble with cramps from the incision in his belly, but the furious pace of reporting boys' and girls' games, back and forth from the *Chronicle's* bullpen editorial offices, obscured his health problems. He worked out, according to Dr. Szezy's instructions, but sporadically. He felt guilty when he missed a planned session. Missing might cost him his varsity slot playing next to Mark. But his responsibilities as the sports reporter were also what he had to do. For that, he needed his own car.

Mom, Dad, and Mark took him to a used car lot in the western end of Landers' Landing, a few blocks from home. Dad had to take title of any purchase, because of Carly's age. They examined several clean looking vehicles, and Carly wanted a 1984 *Firebird*. The front lamp covers were stuck open. Dad settled on an old Ford for the cash Carly had in his account. Mom wrote the check.

With a dealer's sticker on the back window, Carly proudly parked his new car next to Dad's F-150 Lariat and Mark's Clean'Um truck. The vehicles filled in the driveway. Eddie complained he couldn't shoot hoops anymore. Carly moved his car to the street.

After a victorious football game against an out of state high school team, Carly saw Newsom leave the press box. Carly stayed behind and wrote a draft of the game story on an old typewriter. He hacked away when the school's head janitor, Ed Stolley, nudged him in the shoulder.

"I have to turn off the field lights. You'll have to fold."

Scooping up his score card and copy, Carly stashed the material under his arm and went slowly down the stadium bleacher steps. He headed toward the distant parking area for players and officials, turning over in his mind the finishing touches to his story.

As he approached his Ford, he noticed his tires were flat. The motor hood was ajar. He lifted it, and the car's battery was gone. He leaned against the driver's side door. He remembered he had a foot pump in the trunk, but he was stuck without a battery. At least the tires weren't slashed. The vandal had just let out the air.

Using the public phone by the stadium entrance, he called home for Mark, who came in his Clean'Um truck. It nearly got stuck in mud. Its tires shot up globs that spewed over the parking lot in messy strings. They dashed toward downtown and the editorial offices to file the game story on time.

Mark was talkative about his own experience at work. Some lady had invited him inside her house and propositioned him. She'd actually touched him, trying to unzip his pants.

"I can't believe it." Carly said. "Are you going to that address again?"

"She was drunk." Mark shook his head.

Carly's own predicament seemed small by comparison.

"You unlucky guy."

"I know better than to touch somebody in that condition."

"You're a saint."

"A saint I ain't."

Carly's mind was on his own predicament. "Will you drive me out the Interstate truck stop for a battery?"

"I know a better place. They charge too much on the highway."

"What place?"

"A garage near the plant that stays open all night for towing."

They made it to *The Daily Chronicle's* office by 11:00 o'clock. Carly used his key to open the door with the brass mail slot and walked up the long flight of steps.

Newsom worked in the far corner, wearing a Bear's cap. Carly gave him the game story to edit and said that his brother was waiting patiently downstairs. Newsom read the story and nodded, muttering to himself.

"Am I excused?"

Newsom smiled. "Go on. It's just a normal rewrite to fit the headline."

Mark took him to the all-night garage where they picked up a $12.50 used battery. Mark had tools in his truck to help installation. Carly worked the foot pump until the muscles in his incision cramped. Mark gave him a hand and took over. They got home about midnight.

When he told Mom about the vandalism, she shook her head.

"One more expense," she said, as if it were the fault of his employment. She wanted Carly to call the police.

Instead he decided to report the vandalism to the principal's office, since it happened on leased school property.

The next school day, Carly told his principal about the incident. Carly sat in front of Father's impressive desk and coughed up all the details in a rush.

"We may be dealing with a sick person here," Father said.

That was typical, Carly thought. Father almost never *said* exactly what he was *thinking*, which probably was that it's a prank.

"So where do we go from here?"

"The police have instituted a reporting program for incidents on school property. I have a questionnaire for you to fill out. Jurisdiction remains in the school until the problem actually takes on proportions that warrant a police investigation for a specific violation."

"That's what happened to me."

"Then we need to be in touch with the juvenile bureau. Complete the form and I'll refer it for you."

"I'd rather not get involved with the cops."

"I understand, Carly. Complete the form and it'll remain a school matter without a police investigation."

"Can I be excused? I want to talk with my girlfriend, Mary Lou Reiley."

Father smiled. "You're excused."

Carly got up and stood by the chair. He'd gone to confession to Father Alexander almost as much as the pastor, Father Joe.

Confessions always involved his impurities of thought, word and deed. It was a hard sometimes, and it made him reflect. Father wanted details when'd describe his feelings for girls.

He wanted Alexander's blessing on the right thing to do about the vandalism when he talked with his girlfriend. It always flattered Father Alexander to have someone ask for a blessing.

"Can I have your blessing?"

Father motioned for Carly to come around the desk.

He knelt by the side of the armchair and bowed his head.

Father stood and put his hand on Carly's bushy hair.

"Bless this young man in all his endeavors. In the name of the Father, the Son and the Holy Ghost." He made the sign of the cross with his other hand.

Carly got off his knees and towered over his principal.

"I'm sorry I didn't get in to see you when you were hospitalized," Father said. "Are you improving?"

"Yeah, but I don't know when I'll be able to play ball again. It's a real bummer."

Carly appreciated the attention. He held the report form in his hand, turned and left to hunt up Mary Lou.

While he walked down the busy high school hallway, he remembered that he'd kept the incident from her, afraid that she might think badly of him for having an enemy who would commit vandalism.

He saw her standing beside her locker. It was as if she were waiting for him and already knew what to expect.

He launched into a description of the vandalism to his car and Father Alexander's reaction.

"Oh, Carly," she said, taking his arm. "I'm so sorry." She looked at the paper he held in his hand. "Is that the form? Give it to me." She grabbed it and tore it up.

He smiled faintly.

"Just my sentiments."

10

Carly wanted to experiment on a desktop computer in the *Chronicle's* office with a freelance story. He asked Ed Newsom for permission, catching him at a time when the editor was extremely busy. Newsom agreed with a wave of his hand.

"What's the password?"

"Juggernaut."

Sports appeared in a special section of the paper every day, and the need to submit copy drew Carly like a magnet. He made money for every inch published, and it was enough in all to pay for a car, even if the vehicle was old. He used the spell-checker to avoid another letter from Newsom over his atrocious spelling.

The article was about prospects for seniors to get athletic scholarships to big time schools. Carly wrote about Mark's chances for a "letter of intent," as Coach Tuttle put it, to Our Lady University. He brushed over the ethical consideration that he was writing about his kin.

When he finished, he set it aside, because Newsom wanted a preliminary story about the commencement of the upcoming girls' basketball season. Newsom would do the boys' prospects, because Carly expected to be a player.

To add salt to the flavor of the girls' report, Carly went to the girls' coach, Mabel Johnson. She had a small office in the athletic department, far down the hallway from the main complex for the boys. She wore a pair of black cotton pants and a sweatshirt when she met Carly at her office door. A frosted window had inscribed the words *Girls' Sports.*

She unlocked the door and led Carly in with an invitation.

"Come in, dearie."

The office smelled sweet and had one desk, a chair, and a five drawer letter-sized file.

"I only have ten minutes to give you," Mrs. Johnson said.

"My boss at the *Chronicle* wants a preview of the season with an emphasis on the stars."

"I can highlight prospects." Mrs. Johnson sat in the chair.

She reached for the third drawer of the metal file cabinet, pulled the handle and lifted a folder with prepared material. She gave Carly several sheets, including biographies of two players. One was over six feet tall with a 90% free throw average, and the other had a 70% floor shooting record.

"This is the first time the paper has wanted a preseason story," she said. "As you may know, last year we only won a third of the games. But this year will be outstanding."

"How do you account for that?" Carly said, looking around for another folding chair because his belly cramped.

"Several girls from middle school will play first string because of their size," she said. "The Mid-State Catholic Girls' Basketball Conference is in transition. One school is closing, St. Donato's, and another is coming on line, St. Bosco's." She described turmoil in the league.

In ten minutes Carly had enough information for a real potboiler, and he didn't even have to go into the locker room. Mrs. Johnson stood and said she had to leave.

"One other question," Carly said. "How can you direct the proposed school play and be the head girls' basketball coach at the same time?"

"Work. Hard work and careful planning, like every teacher you have in this school, dearie."

Carly had his freelance piece on Newsom's desk the next day. The day after that, Newsom killed it, reminding Carly, in another letter, of journalistic ethics. It was the pits. No publication meant no pay. Perhaps as a consolation, Newsom let the entire 40" length of the girls' basketball story run with a three column headline in *The Sunday Chronicle*.

When Carly showed Newsom's scolding letter to Mary Lou, she called Newsom a dirty old man.

Carly came home from school the day after Columbus Day and found his dad sitting stiffly, wearing a back brace, in his chair in the living room. Mom was standing at the kitchen door, wrenching a wet handkerchief. Dad had been involved in an incident at work.

A fellow worker on a scaffold had lost his footing. Dad had held onto the man, Henry Shafer, until the fire department arrived. The fire chief said Dad's gasping hand had saved Shafer from death. Dad was a hero, but he had to remain confined to home with a back brace and stay away from work for six weeks.

When Mark came home for dinner at 6:00 P.M., he offered to continue employment at the Clean'Um Cleaners into the basketball season. That meant he would have to drop out of varsity basketball. He didn't hesitate.

The only other family income, besides Mom's home party business, would be workers' compensation, when and if it was awarded and commenced payment. Even when Dad's back healed, he might be laid off because of the impending wintertime when outside construction stopped.

Dad accepted Mark's offer. Carly's compensation at *The Daily Chronicle* was scheduled to end in a few more weeks when basketball season started. The need for cash to help Dad came crashing home.

Carly asked his folks for permission to work at Poppachino's Candy Store on non-game Saturdays. They said okay. He mentioned that fact to Jack Mitchem in the hallway. Jack said he was sorry for the old man. The dramatic rescue had made front page news in the paper. Mitchem liked to read bad news.

The candy store owner, "Pops" Poppachino, assigned Carly to what he called the "brown room," a tiny basement storage and sorting facility. Popppachino was a sick man. He was in and out of a wheelchair, which he rolled around his establishment directing others and keeping the business flowing. Often during the day he'd lie down in a back room and catch his breath. Carly was alone to wrap chocolates from inventory into assorted boxes for sale.

The way down was through a hatch in the floor beneath the long busy first floor counter. Carly would've preferred to work at the counter, where he could've met his friends while filling actual sale orders. Poppachino assigned him to the 12 X nine foot pit.

He was inches from shelves containing boxes filled with fine chocolates ordered from Midland at the kitchens of a famous maker in Chicago. He used a stainless steel table for his assembly line and followed instructions on how to sort the "home," "birthday," and "holiday" boxes in one, two and five pound decorated boxes.

There was a tight bathroom where he washed his hands, and a few feet of floor space for maneuvering, which heated rapidly despite a blowing air conditioner. He wore plastic gloves, which quickly darkened with candy, and a thin rubber coverall bib.

Why, he wasn't exactly sure at first, Pudge Roos opened the hatch, stepped down the ladder and closed the cover over her head. She was pleasant and wore a long red-checkered skirt and buttoned blouse.

He always reacted physically to her presence near him, this time with an increase in his rate of breathing. He was surprised. She didn't work at Poppachino's as far as he knew. He guessed what she was after.

"Listen, Pudge, I'm not very horny today."

"Pops needs inventory." She smiled.

She was lying. He breathed faster, more deeply. She was trying another one of her dares. But what?

He reached for a wallphone by the bottom of the ladder. He wanted to confirm her employment. She went about her stated business and took a box of the home collection off a shelf. She paused briefly with her back toward him.

He waited anxiously for Poppachino to answer the phone in his bedroom. There was no immediate pickup. Carly rolled off his dirty plastic gloves.

She turned around. Her blouse was unbuttoned. She exposed her big, flopping breasts and rising nipples. She backed him up to the ladder. The overhead hatch popped open. Jack Mitchem stuck his head down into the hold.

Carly dropped the phone. Suddenly excited, he gasped for breath.

Pudge kissed his lips and rolled her breasts over the flimsy coverall bib. He was aroused.

Mitchem took a flash picture and pulled back. The hatch slammed closed.

Pudge turned, maneuvering around him. She pushed him toward the bathroom doorway, pressing against his back until he reached the bathroom door, which opened to the inside. His heart raced. Beads of sweat came to his forehead. He started to shake.

Next to the door jamb was an open pan of cherry-filled creams. He reached over, grabbing one. He turned around and pushed the cream into her nose. She dropped the box of inventory to the floor.

"You're impossible," she said.

She pulled him back from the doorway and shoved him against a narrow wall. She went into the bathroom and washed the candy off her nose. She sat on the toilet lid, crying while she buttoned her blouse.

He looked at her flushed face, moist cheeks and red eyes. She pushed her arms down between her legs and folded her elbows on her knees. She buried her face in her hands and bawled.

He remembered holding her when they showed each other off after the Midsummer dance. They'd had an even relationship then, but now she was definitely not a partner. He held out his hand to her.

His head swirled. He smelled the fragrance of her body, and he became further aroused.

But he imagined Mitchem's picture being passed around the school surreptitiously with an annexed story of what happened later in the bathroom. He felt his face flush. It felt like when he drank hard liquor down all at once. He looked away.

She reached under his hand, grabbed and twisted his bib. She pressed her head between his legs into his bone.

He had a choice to yield or not to yield.

"I love you," she said. "I love you."

He looked around. He wanted the big one so badly he could taste it. But, holding back, he sighed. He was at Pop's place. Mitchem had the picture. They were involved, and Carly didn't want to be made the butt of their joke.

"Not now," he said. "Not here."

"I'm gonna stop giving you these chances."

"'Kay, 'kay. Let me think."

He weakened. She was a dirty girl. He nearly exploded with passion. More beads of sweat came to his forehead. His chest rocked with the beat of his heart. Everything else faded into obscurity, including his faith.

"We can't do it here," he said.

"What about Bareass's place?"

He froze at the suggestion. But that was the answer.

People called Tom Bareschitz, Bareass. He was the permanent kitchen help at Poppachino's, and he lived alone in a downtown apartment. He would rent the place to couples, when he liked them, to "sort of get them started in life." He offered his bed, clean sheets and towels, a bath, and TV VCR with pornographic videos for a total hourly rent of fifty dollars. His business was among kids, who guarded the operation like a secret from adults.

Pudge released his bib. She grazed her hand over his pants, petting him, and drew back her head. She stood and passed him out the bathroom doorway. She went to the ladder and paused, checking her blouse.

He turned and watched her progress to the ladder, but he only went forward a step outside the bathroom. His shoe pushed against the dropped box of chocolates. His arousal faded.

Pudge flipped up the back of her long checkered skirt. She squatted, holding the skirt up.

He was stunned again. She had no underwear. She stuck out her butt and wiggled like a bawdy maiden, mooning his direction.

"Later, Pudge."

She climbed up the ladder steps. She looked like a muscled, prowling cougar. She lifted the hatch, jumped up and let the cover fall back with a slam.

He went over to the ladder, picked up the phone receiver and listened. It was dead. He replaced it on the wall's hook.

He reached for a clean pair of plastic gloves. When he put them on, he turned to the stainless table and spread his hands on the top. He had to steady himself. He was shaking. His legs trembled.

He meant to do it, the big one, but not in this place. It had the potential to turn him on his head.

He picked up the chocolate box she'd dropped when he squashed a cherry cream in her nose. He ripped it open and stuffed a bunch in his mouth. The chocolates filled his throat, and he paused. It really tasted good.

That was it. That's how he'd gain weight.

11

Later Saturday, Carly checked with Tom Bareschitz about what happened. Bareschitz said that Mitchem had set up Pudge. He'd teased her to go after her prey and taken the picture with the cooperation of the counter people. They were all in on the big practical joke except the boss.

The next time at work, always the salesman, Bareschitz gave Carly an *Ever-Bloom* book of pinups. It showed all kinds of positions for sexual intercourse between a male and a female. Bareschitz followed up with an offer to show Carly his place, which was down the street in "old downtown" Landers' Landing.

"When you pay me fifty bucks, I'll go someplace else for an hour," Bareschitz said while he was pealing potatoes in Poppachino's kitchen. "All you have to do is signal you're still inside. Put a pillow in front of the door. You'll be left undisturbed."

Later, Carly followed Bareschitz up three flights of stairs and into his set of two rooms and a bath. The living room floor gave with a snap from Carly's step. He looked around for any TV VCR remote, found one on the spongy sofa and switched it on. One of the videos was already inserted. The quality was grainy. The action, boys with boys, was unlike what Carly expected.

Bareschitz was a homo.

Carly shut off the TV VCR. He went into the bedroom and sat on the springy mattress.

Bareschitz went into the bathroom and pissed. Carly saw him come out with a can of scent, which he sprayed around the bedroom. He was a short, bony guy, with a small, uneven mustache and beady eyes. He was six years out of high school and had been with Poppachino for all six.

"You're the second Nichols kid I've had in here," he said.

Carly was puzzled.

"You didn't know Markie came up for some ass?"

Bareschitz tossed the can of scent across the room to a 30 gallon plastic garbage container.

Carly felt his face blush.

It was true. Mark was not a virgin. He was the first to make the big one. But Carly thought it happened in her car, whoever she was.

"Who was it you ask?"

Carly nodded.

"Fudge, you know, the one Mitchem photographed. Boy, did they stay a long time. I came back three times and the pillow was still there. I charged them extra."

Carly stood.

His head spun with little shooting stars going every which way. He'd traveled the same road into lust that Mark had laid out.

He coughed like he was embarrassed. His belly went tight. He started to feel aroused.

"Here's **your** chance, Carly," he remembered Pudge saying after the Fall Ball. She'd meant here's your chance after Mark.

"I'm gonna stop giving **you** these chances," he remembered her saying after her attack in the brown room. His, after Mark's, is what she meant, using a little female ambiguity.

"I've seen enough," Carly said, looking around the dingy rooms. "I'll let you know."

He brought home the *EverBloom* and stuffed it in his box file beneath his bedroom bunk, but he recognized what was happening: his emotions were running wild.

The next morning was Sunday. He wanted to go to confession before the early Mass. He slipped through the side doorway of St. Andrew's, genuflected, and prepared for the sacrament of reconciliation with prayers and an examination of conscience.

He took his place by the confessional door. No one was ahead of him. Father Joe had been Carly's frequent companion for basketball in the gym after school, but Carly felt he had to have a discussion about his frustrating and complicated passion despite any lack of anonymity.

The priest came through the side doorway from the rectory. He wore a black cassock, nodded at Carly, opened the middle confessional door and sat between the penitents' booths. He switched on a green light over the penitents' doors.

Carly looked at flickering candles lighting a votive stand. They created a soft orange illuminating glow while he opened the door to a booth and knelt. He listened to his own breathing and faced a screened divider in the darkness. A panel behind a little screen door by his mouth slid open. Father Joe was ready.

Carly sighed.

"Bless me, Father, for I have sinned. I lied once and disobeyed once, and I had impure thoughts about a girl."

He knew Father Joe was interested in which sex he focused his attention. He'd deliberately said *girl* instead of leaving the object open with "impure thoughts" period.

"Are you sorry?"

Carly had to think about that. The lie was a little one, telling his mother he had no trouble at Poppachino's working in the basement. The disobedience was slightly bigger, not following Doctor Szezy's order on exercising. But the impurity of thought masked his real desire.

Gradually, he came to the conclusion that Father Joe was holding him up, wanting to hear more details.

"Can you undo the disobedience and take back the lie?"

"Not really, Father. Aren't you more concerned with my thoughts about the girl?"

"Are you willing to tell me a little bit more?"

"I'd rather not. I want absolution."

After all, Father Joe was Coach Tuttle's twin brother. While it was discrimination for anyone to be thrown off the squad for immorality, it could be the subject of discipline.

"I see," Father Joe said.

"It's very hard for me, putting my feelings for this girl into words."

"I take it you were very aroused."

"She exposed herself to me. I know she's the occasion of sin, but I'm attracted."

"Do you love her? Are you planning a future with her?"

"I like her."

"It's not a sin to like someone." Father sounded annoyed.

"I imagine us together. It's consuming me. What can I do about it, besides the obvious?"

Father Joe paused.

"Who's your favorite saint?" he said.

"St. Francis."

"Try to imitate him. He was an inspiring person, and his life has been an example for countless boys."

"That's a good idea," Carly said. He paused. He remembered his doctor's advice to gain weight and get back his muscle tone, which was cultivating his body. "I read a biography about him. He prayed so much he got scum on his knees. He starved his body with fasting. My doctor says I have to eat more and improve my muscle tone."

"Are you recovering from an illness?"

Father Joe was trying to be considerate by ignoring what he had to know about Carly's injury.

"I guess you could say that."

"Think how Jesus wants you to imitate him. Keep in shape with Jesus in mind."

"'Kay. I'm really trying."

"I'll give you absolution now. For your penance say three Hail Marys and three Our Fathers."

12

At noon Sunday, Jack Mitchem called to see whether Carly would be interested in going to the last day of outdoor roller skating at the rink before winter closed in.

"You've got a lot of nerve after what you did at Pop's," Carly said. "I don't think I'd be interested."

"Want your picture?"

"What are you suggesting?"

"You can have the negative for a few bucks."

"All right."

"I'll pick you up at your house at one. Bring as much money as you can."

On the way to the rink in Mitchem's folks' SUV, Mitchem talked about a party at the rink, mostly of female students from St. Basil's. After parking, they entered the boys' hut, which rested at one end of the rink opposite the girls' hut. There was a chimney pipe over a smudge pot in the winter when the rink was covered in ice. The park commission policed the rink. The previous year the commissioners had divided one hut after a nasty incident when a fight had developed between boys and girls changing shoes in the same hut. The result was cramped, separate quarters for each sex.

Carly wore a Bull's knitted cap, which he pulled down to his eyebrows. Mitchem whistled. They sat on a wooden bench while putting on their skates. Mitchem had mentioned nothing more about selling Carly the negative. Carly figured the first person to bring up the deal would be at an advantage.

He stopped Mitchem at the hut's doorway, just as they were about to slide out onto the concrete pad. Carly took out his wallet and gave Mitchem his last 15 dollars.

Mitchem grabbed it and gave him an envelope. Carly stuffed it in his pocket. He breathed a sigh of relief and rolled onto the rink.

Skating was good for his belly. The exercise took his mind off his problems, like Father Joe wanted. He sighted Mary Lou Reiley emerging from the girls' hut.

"Hey Mitch, look over there. It's Lou and her gang." He saw at least six other juniors around Mary Lou.

Junior girls giggled and talked in a bunch. From Carly's viewpoint in a neutral zone far away, he saw a big fat boy, Leon Sweeney, one of Mitchem's pals, trip against the whole gang. They fell.

Suddenly Carly heard a yell like a wounded cat. He'd know Mary Lou's voice anywhere. He raced over to the stricken girls.

"I didn't mean to fall on her," someone said. She started to cry in staccato sobs. "I'm sorry, I'm sorry."

The scene looked disastrous. Those pushed down struggled to get up. Under the bottom of the pile lay Mary Lou Reiley. She was crumpled and groaning, unable to get up on her own.

Carly shoved into the crowd and knelt down by her side. He saw her bruised leg.

It had long doubled up stockings, and he tried to move her, but she wouldn't let him. Her soft dark hair spread out in waves over her face and down onto the shoulders. He bunched her hair, took off his cap, and folded the hair inside the knitting. He pulled the cap down.

Tears streamed over her rosy cheeks, making lines of black mascara from her eyelids.

"I'm just bruised," she said after a moment. "Nothing broken, nothing cut."

She took Carly's hand and pulled herself up. She held on tightly but slipped on the roller skates. He hugged her. She stood straight.

Others milled about. Carly heard people blaming each other for bunching up, falling down together and for drinking too much at Sunday brunch. Apparently they were not all aware of Leon Sweeney's fall which had cascaded them to the ice.

Like a pubescent kid, Sweeney had run away from the gang toward Mitchem. They went into the boys' hut and Carly saw them change shoes, go the SUV and leave the lot. Mitchem screeched the tires when he left.

After the rink cleared, Carly realized that Mitchem hadn't come back for him. The girls went home, leaving him alone. Mary Lou still had his cap.

A few minutes later, Mitchem's SUV pulled up along side the hut. Mitchem rolled down his window.

"Hop in."

"Where'd you take Leon?" Carly swung into the passenger bucket seat.

"Home. He was scared."

"It looked to me like he tripped the girls."

Mitchem grinned. "Not that they didn't deserve it."

"That's crazy, Jack."

"It should crimp the style of the most popular womb in the junior class." Mitchem made it sound like Mary Lou deserved punishment. If he enjoyed something like that, he was not only mixed up but malicious.

"You're talking about my girlfriend."

"No offense intended." Mitchem smiled. The pimples on his cheek tightened, and one began to leak pus.

Carly reached over and swiped it. Jack drew back, frowning. "I wonder about you, boy."

"I wonder about you, Jack."

Mitchem arrived in front of the Nichols' house on Grove Avenue. He was six inches shorter than Carly, but he was breathing hard after his remark about referring to Mary Lou as a womb.

Putting down girls gave Mitchem pleasure. It was more intense than teasing. Carly had heard him refer to girls as *holes*, and maybe womb was an improvement on that. He was terribly insecure with either sex. A boy would be an *asshole*. He seem to feel big when he slighted anyone. It bolstered his ego to make light of those around him. He'd try to pass off the attitude as darkly humorous.

Carly climbed out of the SUV. Mitchem drove away but looked back. Carly thought he was grimacing, as if he were sorry for the sexual reference to Mary Lou.

Mitchem was always sorry, later.

On the curb outside his house, Carly dug out from his pocket the envelope containing the negative. Pudge's breasts appeared like white medallions in the black background. The top of Carly's head looked bushy. He saw the knot of the bib coverall tied around his neck. He saw his own hand reaching, grasping toward Pudge. He slipped the negative back into the envelope and stuffed it in his pocket. He wanted to keep it with him, but he asked, Would St. Francis carry around such a thing?

St. Francis stripped naked in his village square.

Inside he called Mary Lou's house, but her mother said she was sedated and sleeping. He should call back the next day.

The next day after school, Carly went to her house. She was absent all day and he had to see her about his cap, her wound and the essay contest. Her mother showed him into the living room, where Mary Lou was sitting on a couch. She seemed glad to see him, gave him his cap and wanted him sit beside her. Their backs would be toward the greenhouse door.

He let himself down carefully. He didn't want to jar her bruised leg, but she winced anyhow. She was still sore from tumbling to the floor of the skating rink.

He wore his old Lettermen's Club jacket from the sophomore year, but the year's letters were torn off. His entry in the National Catholic Essay Contest was sticking out of the left pocket. He noticed that she was working on her contest entry.

"Do you know who fell against you yesterday?" he said. "It was Leon Sweeney. It looked like he deliberately tripped."

He took out his contest entry.

"I hardly know Leon Sweeney. He's a big fat smelly pig."

"He did it."

"Well, I can't do anything about that."

"You could report it to Father Alexander, if you think it was deliberate."

"You know, that's a shitty idea. It didn't happen on school property, and Father could bring in the juvenile bureau. Have you ever been down there? It's a zoo."

"Let's talk about the essay contest," he said, sorry he brought up the other subject. "Did you see from the date on the entry form that the results will be back about the time they elect the editor-in-chief of the *Beam*?"

She pinched his cheek. He was glad he'd shaved in the morning. She kissed him softly on the cheek and handed him her essay.

He read it as a homily to a saint. It was written like a ritual consisting of prayers and devotions on various days of the week. Even though saints had been invoking the Christian spirit on the earth for two thousand years, hers had originality, he thought.

"You're a real writer."

"Gimme yours." She grabbed it from his hand. She also poked his ribs.

He tightened his diaphragm, but when she nudged him it really didn't hurt.

She read his essay silently and looked into his face.

"It's what you might expect from a 16-year-old boy."

He folded her presentation and slapped her arm gently with it.

Carly heard the greenhouse door squeak behind him. He looked around and saw her dad holding a baby coon in one hand, stroking its fur with the other. He wore a rubber waist bib, gloves and long sleeves.

Carly stood and looked at her dad. He had the bushiest eyebrows he'd ever seen, perched above cool green eyes. His head was mainly bald but had strands of white hair over a freckled surface. His bulbous nose was striped with blood vessels.

Carly stood at attention. "Hello, sir."

"Thank you for helping my daughter at the rink yesterday."

"My pleasure, sir." Carly smiled.

Mr. Reiley abruptly turned around and walked toward the greenhouse doorway, petting his baby coon.

Carly felt relieved after meeting the big booster, fine Catholic gentleman and wild pet fancier.

Mr. Reiley closed the greenhouse door gently.

Mary Lou kissed Carly again, this time on the lips. She looked over his ragged jacket. She looked like she wanted it.

"Can I give you my jacket?"

"I'd rather have a Lettermen's Club jacket."

"This is a lettermen's jacket. I just took off the letters."

She must have known about his entitlement. "I mean something newer." She sighed. She looked disgusted with him on the subject to clothes. "Do you even have a suit to wear?"

"I can get one, if it's important to you."

She turned away. "Oh, don't bother."

He leaned toward her. "Is there anything else I can get for you?"

She turned back and smiled. She shook her head. They both stood, and he stuffed his essay into his back pocket. He walked beside her down the long entrance hallway with the wall clock, mail table and hat tree to the vestibule door.

They kissed for a long, affectionate moment, twisting the process. His essay popped out of his pocket, and he picked it up.

"I'll call you in the morning," she said.

Outside, he looked around the sumptuous, landscaped lawn over to the dark catalpa tree with its spiny seeds. The Reiley house and yard were ten times bigger than his folks' humble bungalow.

He could learn to be at ease in such a fine neighborhood. His plans for using the Reiley family to advance his own ambitions and gain the love of the Irish virgin were still in place, if he didn't dislodge them by going off with Pudge to Bareass's place.

He went to his old Ford with its fosted front window. He drew a finger in the film of the window into the form of a Cupid's heart and arrow and drove home.

Mary Lou called when he arrived. She said she couldn't wait until the morning to talk to him again. She told him how surprised she was that her dad had broken into their conversation while he was feeding his pets. She told him he shouldn't be shy about coming over to see him even if her dad was around the house.

He wondered why she was so defensive. It was overnight before he realized that she'd probably made it clear to her dad that Carly was her guy.

She was good for him. She wanted him to buy his first suit, and she probably had something specific in find for him to wear it at.

Since he'd be going to college, he had to have a decent wardrobe. Mark had a suit. Dad had a suit. Only he and Eddie didn't have suits yet. One had to be prepared for things like social fraternities, dinners and dances.

13

In the morning Carly cornered Mark after chemistry class.

"Look what I've got," Mark said before Carly could ask about suits available from the cleaners. Mark showed him letter-sized drawings of little chemical structures. "Notice the difference between the two?"

Carly looked and shook his head. Underneath each drawing was either sodium chloride or potassium nitrate. He laughed.

"Salt and saltpeter."

"I've been to the kitchen, and it was the latter. Bright boy."

Carly asked about the men's suits from inventory at Clean'Um. Mark said the only ones available were so badly stained that customers refused to accept them back. Even those suits cost $10 apiece, the price of the cleaning job.

Stained suits. What was it like, Markie, taking Pudge Roos to Tom Bareschitz's rooms and getting naked? What happened, Markie, when Bareass came back and found the pillow still by the door three times? Why pass off the fucking as happening in the back seat of someone's car, Markie?

"What do you need a suit for?"

Outside the chemistry laboratory the smell wafted from an open door, and kids carrying lab workbooks passed them by.

"Oh, nothing. Just in case, I suppose," Carly said, looking down.

"Don't you have money from your newspaper job to buy a good suit at Emerald's Gentlemen's Wear in the westside mall?"

"I tell you, Markie, my car takes everything I've got, except for what I contribute to Mom and Dad. That's really why I'm working at Pops' place. It isn't just for Mom and Dad like you."

Mark thought about that for a moment. He looked like he knew what was bothering Carly, who never complained.

"I've got a proposition for you, bro. Let's go on a double date to the Grotto of Saint Joseph before winter closes in. My treat."

"It'll have to be Sunday afternoon." Carly looked up into Mark's unshaven face. "Who would you take?"

"Melody." He smiled as if he were in the throes of love.

Of course Mark wouldn't take Pudge. He'd dropped her, just like Carly had, when she became the occasion of sin.

"'Kay. Mary Lou would enjoy that. I would, too."

"We can have a sandwich at the diner in Edwardsville and take in a movie at the drive-in that's between the town and the grotto. The last shows before winter are this weekend."

Carly nodded.

After making the double date, Carly didn't want any cheap ten dollar wonder from Clean'Um. He also didn't follow up on Mark's suggestion of Emerald's at westside because of lack of funds.

He went to the rummage closet with Mom. The place was operated by the St. Andrew's Parish Ladies' Sodality. He found a tall dark suit for free, but it smelled. He paid Mark to have dry cleaning done at work, and he was ready for whatever Mary Lou had in mind.

After Mark dropped off the cleaned suit in the living room at home, Carly took it into his bedroom to hang it up in the closet. He saw Eddie looking at his *EverBloom* photogravure.

Eddie slumped over the edge of Carly's bed, the lower bunk, with Carly's private file box between his sneakers. Coach Tuttle's book of plays, on loan from Mark, was in Eddie's lap. The magazine was in his hands.

"What are you doing?" Carly said.

Eddie held up the picture book of pinups. It was turned open to a salacious page of pink-colored flesh. His face filled with a glistening bright red color. He pushed the pages closed and dropped the *EverBloom* into Carly's box.

Carly slid the suit on top of Eddie's mattress next to the ladder and sat on his own bunk next to Eddie.

"What can I say, Eddie? You've been in my private file. Do I go into your private file?"

Eddie clutched the book of plays on his lap. "I wanted to see Coach Tuttle's plays. It was underneath."

"Bareass gave it to me. He's peddling his apartment for rendezvous."

"The guy at Pops'?"

"The same. Poppachino's pimp."

"Are you finished with it? I know some people who'd like to see it. You know I have a girlfriend now."

"Well, I don't think you should be passing it around to your friends."

"Her name is Hastie McFarland." Eddie smiled.

Carly recognized her name and thought he knew what she looked like. She had prominent freckles on her face and red hair. She lived in a house with a chain fence around several hound dogs in the back yard. He didn't know whether she was nice, but the fact that Eddie wanted to show her the *EverBloom* didn't bode like a beacon. She certainly was pretty. Like Mary Lou, a fetching Irish virgin?

Carly sighed. He used Mary Lou's phrase to show his exasperation.

"This is going nowhere, Eddie. If you want to keep it, 'Kay. They're just pictures. If you want my opinion, it's a marriage manual. You're a long way from getting married."

"I'll stay out of your file in the future, but can I at least look at Coach Tuttle's plays?"

"Sure."

Eddie folded up the play book and put it under his arm.

"I'm sorry I got into your file without asking."

Eddie stood, kicked Carly's box under the bunk and swung himself to the top bunk with one foot on the second rung of the ladder. He settled in to read the basketball plays.

Carly took his suit to the closet, leaving the *EverBloom* in his box, and went out of the bedroom. He passed from the living room, where Dad was sleeping in front of the TV, into the kitchen and out the back door. He went to the trash barrel behind the garage. He started a fire with twigs. He wondered a moment whether he should pitch and burn the pinups, allowing them to be consumed like the fires of hell. But he didn't go back inside and get the pictures. He let them lie like sleeping dogs.

He went back inside and sat on the sofa next to his dad's chair. Dad held the TV remote in his lap. Many times the old man had told everyone at dinner how he'd fallen in love with Mom, attracted by her bright eyes, her physical energy and her intelligence.

They were both interned at the Catholic orphanage under the care of sisters. He'd known her for years before he'd become attracted when he was about sixteen. Right after the orphanage, Dad started with the Pieper Building Company. He'd earned big bucks working night and day on a highway paving crew. They'd married in the church and had Mark right away, exactly nine months later. Carly and Eddie had come along in rapid order.

Then something had happened, and they had had no more kids. Dad explained one night at the dinner table, in the presence of all three boys, who were in middle school at the time.

"The rhythm method. Every one of you boys needs to understand how that works."

"How does it work?" Mark said.

"You just have to count the days from the end of the girl's menstrual cycle forward two weeks. That's the only time she's fertile. She has to keep a calendar. Make sure your dates keep a calendar. I know how it is to be a kid."

"We shouldn't be discussing this at the table," Mom said.

"It's all right," Mark said. "I'm interested. I don't want Dad to feel he's out of line."

"I'm interested, too," Carly said.

"Me, too," Eddie said.

"Dad's never out of line," Mom said. "But sometimes he's a bit too frank in his appraisal of what needs to be said to you boys as a group."

Carly drove Mary Lou's family's SUV on the double date to the Grotto of Saint Joseph near Edwardsville. The shrine was a famous wayside stop visited by thousands each year, even though it was off the state highway two miles on a county road. It was beside a church with a vaulted ceiling and tapered spire that used to have a permanent pastoral assignment. After Vatican II, attendance had withered. The parish became first a mission, then closed and was "purged," as the bishop's order in the Catholic paper had read.

That was the first time Carly had heard of a church closing. He thought, as Christ's home, churches always lasted forever, except in early times when the Huns raided Rome.

It was two miles away from the drive-in on the state highway with the only remaining outdoor movie screen that Carly knew of. They would have supper in Edwardsville, pay homage to Saint Joseph, turn the car back down the road and see the current exploitation, or B film, without spending a lot of Mark's money.

Eddie wanted to go along with Hastie McFarland. He had a handheld travel game and said the boys should all go together and play it. Carly pointed out that it would take a bus to transport everyone. That was when Carly got Mary Lou to provide her folks' SUV with a full tank of gas.

Every girl in the SUV had freckles in the face. Every boy was a Nichols. The trip ended when the old SUV split an engine hose along the state highway.

Everyone climbed out of the SUV and stood on the roadside in the Sunday afternoon breeze while traffic whizzed by. Mark diagnosed the problem immediately. He tried to tie off the hose with his handkerchief, but it was insufficient.

Melody Malone had the saving suggestion. She wore a skirt with pantyhose. She offered to use her hose to tie off the leak.

Mark got a plastic pail painted "Tolly" from the floor of the back seat of the SUV. He went to a stream next to the adjacent field of harvested soybeans and scooped water to replace the lost radiator fluid. Melody went behind the SUV and peeled her pantyhose.

Carly sensed that the informality of Melody and Mark suggested physical love. Mark smelled the pantyhose when he prepared to wrap the stocking around the radiator hose. Melody had nothing for a replacement.

Mark's repair was temporary. They either had to find a station to replace the split hose or keep filling the radiator every five minutes. By the time the attendant in an Edwardsville shop completed the replacement, it was dark. Melody found new hose at a drug store. The final movie eight miles away had started. The grotto wasn't lighted at night. They all ate hamburgers, on Mark, in a local café before heading home.

Mark's 18th birthday came. It promised to be an exciting event because of a secret, which Dad was not keeping very well.

When Carly got home from school, Mom wanted him to run to the store for vanilla extract. Eddie tagged along.

"Mark's going to get the Pieper Scholarship," Eddie said, putting his fingers perpendicular to his lips.

So Mark's sacrifice of varsity basketball on the altar of family welfare had a material reward after all.

When Carly and Eddie returned with the flavoring, Mom was garnishing the chuck roast. The incredibly beefy odor filled the kitchen. Mom made the frosting for the cake. Everyone sat on kitchen chairs at 6:00 P.M. for dinner.

After a rousing chorus of *Happy Birthday to You*, Mom gave her present to Mark. It was a book a Psalms, which Mark had requested. Then Dad made his announcement.

Mom let out a little yelp and clapped her hands. Carly and Eddie jointed in the appleause.

"Well, thanks Dad," Mark said.

The award was related to Dad's injury. The Pieper Building Company gave out annual scholarships in the name of deserving employees for their families near the end of the construction season. It was endowed, and not dependent on how well the company performed any particular year, but it was usually given only to heroes like their father. That year, for saving Henry Shafer's life, the hero's cowl fell on Dad Nichols' designee, his oldest son Mark. He was slated to receive a full tuition, room and board scholarship grant annually for the next four years, provided it was to a Catholic University.

"Our Lady U.," Mark announced.

Later that night, Carly asked Mark what he was going to major in at Our Lady University now that he didn't have to accept an athletic scholarship for basketball.

"Philosophy," Mark said.

Did Mark need to serve God? When he was growing up, he didn't always follow everything in the Bible and what the Roman Catholic Church taught him in his Catholic school education. He had that experience with Pudge Roos at the Bareass barn. Yet his latest birthday present was Psalms. He did enjoy the liturgy. He regularly attended Mass and tried to follow the teachings of the church. Except for his slip with Pudge, he'd lived a clean life and had a reputation as a leader.

When the opportunity arose for a tryst with a woman Clean'um customer, he said he was attracted. He'd probably had a few other requests, too. But the woman happened to stink from alcohol rather than smell of perfume. He wanted a woman his way. He wanted life his way.

14

Mary Lou's mom opened the front door to Carly the next day. Mrs. Reiley had a squeaky voice, but it seemed ingratiating. She wore a suit as if preparing to go out. It was easy to see where Mary Lou got her charms. Carly was there to pick her up for school and had a box of chocolates under his arm.

"Just go right upstairs," Mrs. Reiley said. "I think she's studying." She stared at the decorated box under his arm.

He wore a new Lettermen's Club jacket, which the members allowed him to purchase on the basis of the one football game he played in August. He dashed up the steps, two at a time, having gotten back his old vigor. His muscle tone was greatly improved with all the running around he'd done as a reporter. It was weeks since he'd seen any bleeding from his belly, and days since he'd experienced any pain from the incision.

At the top of the steps he looked around the carpeted landing and down a long hallway with many closed doors. He realized he didn't know where Mary Lou's bedroom was.

"Lou?" he called out.

"In here."

He was standing directly in front of her door. He opened it gently. He saw a four poster bed trimmed in lace, a dark mahogany dresser, a hope chest, stereo, pink wallpaper, a fancy ceiling fan and darkly tufted carpet. She sat in front of a folded open secretary-style desk. He walked in and handed her the home box of chocolates wrapped in a yellow ribbon.

"How sweet," she said. She ripped off the wrapping he had spent five minutes putting together with tape. "You shouldn't have. I'll be as big as a balloon." She lifted the lid.

"Not you," Carly said, thinking of her bony hips. "Ready?"

"Mom's taking me to brunch with some of her country club friends, so I'm skipping this morning," she said. "I'm sorry I didn't call you. But I'm scared what's going to happen at the election tomorrow. I've got to calm down."

He took off his Lettermen's Club jacket and handed it to her anyway, then incongruously blurted out about Mark's scholarship grant.

"He's going to major in philosophy at Our Lady U. I think he wants to devote himself to God."

"I always thought priests had it pretty cushy. Anyway, I know they've got a monopoly."

"Don't think I have any such inclinations."

"I did mentioned that once, didn't I?"

She offered him a chocolate, then accepted his jacket and set it on top of the gift box at the side of her desk.

They went together to Sister Virginia's journalism class for the election of the next editor-in-chief of the *St. Basil Beam*. Over in a rear corner of the classroom were the visible trappings of the out-going *Beam* editorial staff: a rolltop editor's desk, two stacks of file boxes and a drafting board.

Carly sat next to Mary Lou. Out of the gate, he nominated her, got a second and moved the nominations be closed.

Sister Virginia explained that the rules were changed from the previous year at the last minute. The old rule was that a winner needed a majority vote of those attending. Sister said that Father Alexander had newly requested that several candidates' names be submitted to him for final approval. That, she explained, was because Father held a veto power, owing to the monetary aspects of the job. The principal had to sign every work order to make the contract valid for the underage kids running the project.

The person empowered by the principal would take office immediately, but the first issue under the new regime wouldn't be actually published until after New Year's.

The journalism students stirred with the disclosure that they had a contest for the new chief. Sister Virginia adjourned for members of the class to decide nominations. Cliques formed.

Three names besides Mary Lou Reiley were offered: Melody Malone, Jack Mitchem and Pudge Roos. Mary Lou had a fight on her hands. Sister Virginia asked each nominee to make a statement before the secret voting. Two names would be passed on to the principal.

Mary Lou came prepared with big plans for altering the status quo. She excelled with her preciseness. She had an independence of opinion Carly felt he lacked. He thought Jack Mitchem and Pudge Roos would finish in a tie for last, and the real competition was between Mary Lou and Melody Malone.

He was right about the outcome. The names submitted were hers and Melody's. Father's choice would be announced the next day in class.

Carly held hands with Mary Lou after school and at her house that afternoon. Under the new Lettermen's Club jacket, she curled up on the carpet in front of her folks' gigantic projection TV set and watched sitcoms. Carly stretched out beside her. He thought she was upset by the change in the voting rules, and he wanted to comfort her.

He moved in close. She kissed him, and he kissed her all over her face and neck. They embraced. He moved around on the carpet, catching his pants in the tufts. The pants slid down slightly. Mary Lou closed her eyes and made a humming sound.

That was progress. He glowed with her response. He felt wonderful touching her.

He was just about to put his hand on her bosom when her brother, Tolly, and her sister, Molly, showed up from the back of the house. The kids came in the living room like a stampeding herd of buffaloes. They circled, holding hands over their mouths, and, while they squealed and jumped, pointed their fingers at Carly and Mary Lou.

Carly stood.

With his big blue eyes, Tolly looked up.

"Boy, you're tall!"

Tolly menacingly opened his mouth and wiggled his tongue.

"I was just leaving," Carly said, hitching his pants.

Father Alexander appointed Mary Lou to fill the job of editor-in-chief.

She wanted to release the story to *The Daily Chronicle*. It was also Carly's last day as the school sports' correspondent. He had to turn in his pamphlets to Ed Newsom. She told him to write her story while he was down there.

In the editorial bullpen before talking with Newsom, Carly typed a news release about her election. He asked Wendell Tank, the city editor, if he would be interested in running the story. Tank smiled, took the release from Carly's hand and referred him to Newsom for some reason.

Carly heard the presses start up downstairs in production. He saw Newsom, wearing a Bull's cap, hacking away with two sheets of newsprint in an old typewriter. He only did that when he was really upset at something.

The owner of the paper, Max Abel, opened the door to his private office and signaled to Newsom. Able was a short, wizened old man. Carly was between him and Newsom in the bullpen, in a perfect position to watch what followed. He overheard what Able said.

"This is the printout of our inventory in storage." He held the papers and pointed toward Carly. "Go over it with the young man, Ed."

Newsom went to his boss, waddling from his jock itch and hemorrhoids, and took the papers. While he scratched himself on the way back to his desk, he gave them to Carly.

Able waved at Carly and went back into his office, closing the door. Carly noticed him standing inside by the window which overlooked the editorial office and smiling.

Carly sat in front of Newsom's desk.

"The publisher has certain reconditioned machines and equipment," Newsom said. "They're retired articles located in a storage room."

Carly reviewed the inventory. A minimal list of sought-after articles consisted of a copier, metal file drawers, a paper cutter, a camera and an enlarger.

"Can I see them?"

Newsom stood, and, as he did, Carly looked at the story in his old typewriter. It was a letter addressed to him thanking him for service over the past two months and wishing him luck in the future. Carly took his pamphlets out of his pocket and set them over Newsom's desk with the press card. Newsom yanked the letter from his typewriter and gave it to Carly after signing it.

They went to the storage room downstairs. It was by the roaring presses. Carly merely took notes on needed articles and what else might please Mary Lou. Included were folding metal chairs, curtains, tables, and computers, printers and monitors.

There was no restriction on what was available from the retired materials. Carly marked the inventory list, intending to call for her okay before he left the newspaper building.

When he called her, he learned that her dad had arranged for the use of the articles with publisher Able. She approved all the items he checked on the inventory list. He was supposed to tag the items until she decided when and how they would be moved, and to exactly where at the high school.

To accept big donations like the journalism equipment, the school's board of directors had to pass a resolution. Mary Lou asked Carly to go with her to see Father Alexander. He thought it was to arrange that permission. On the way to the principal's office, she asked Carly to be her assistant editor-in-chief, "in charge of all lower ranking minions."

"You know I'll be starting basketball next week," he said. "I'll be your assistant, if you understand I can't be around all the time."

She frowned. They went into the principal's office, passing Ellie Blancard who flagged them in. Father gave Mary Lou the board's resolution of permission to accept the donations of *The Daily Chronicle*. He seemed glad that her dad, a member of the board, had arranged the whole setup, probably at her request.

The resolution established the value of articles for purposes of a tax deduction from the *Chronicle's* income. Carly wondered where all the stuff was going to be put.

"We're in dire additional need," Mary Lou said to Father. "The previous editors used Sister's room. I want a separate workroom, possibly 'C' on the third floor for all the new stuff and my staff. Isn't that reasonable?"

Father rocked his armchair while he looked over the long list of donations. Mary Lou looked at Carly, and Carly looked at her smiling and pleased that she knew to provide a place.

"You'll need Ed Stolley's help," Father said.

Big Ed Stolley was the school's head janitor. He was known as a snitch. Stolley routinely checked wastebaskets and kitchen garbage for deposit containers he could return for the nickel refund, and for other items such as cigarette butts, beer bottles and condoms. He reported his findings to Ellie Blanchard on a piece of paper, which everyone in school knew as the *Deep Shit Report*. Jack Mitchem had several items traced to him, and they weren't soda cans. The school allowed Stolley to retain the cash refunds on any containers he located.

"After you see Ed, put some paint on the walls," Father said, looking at Carly. "I might even be able to wrangle a professional sign painter to scroll 'Editorial Offices' across the door. I know a parent who owes me a favor."

"Father," Mary Lou said, "you are a great man."

Father smiled, obviously pleased with the flattery.

15

The new *Beam* establishment opened the next day. Ed Stolley placed a dozen banker's boxes against the wall by the door that led to the new office next to a box of plastic garbage bags. Mary Lou had the key. Carly followed her inside. The room smelled. It was jammed with broken furniture, stacked books, papers and refuse and the school building was only ten years old. Mary Lou started to sort the material.

"This is disgusting," she said. She ran her fingers over the dust on a Ditto machine. "All right, Carly Nichols. I'll give you a chance to name a person to the staff if you'll see to cleaning up the place."

It naturally occurred to him to name Eddie to a post. The business manager's position would be a new direction for Eddie, away from pornography and girls, and toward developing his place in the world. It was perfect because working for the *Beam* would give him some responsibility.

"My brother Eddie for business manager," he said.

She had no reaction to his nepotism. He had no guilt feeling like when Newsom rejected his article extolling Mark as a hotshot basketball player. But her lack of reaction dragged on for a moment.

"If you don't mind," he said.

"Is he as good as you are?"

"We have the same inclinations."

They discussed Eddie's chores if he accepted the position. Carly said he would explain it all to his little brother.

At home in bed that night, Carly asked Eddie, who was in bed in the upper bunk, whether he would be interested. Carly explained that the editor-in-chief wanted to put the *Beam* on a sound financial footing.

"What would I have to do?"

"Actually, the job of business manager has three aspects. The first is raising money through advertising sales. The second is getting Father Alexander to approve work orders. The third is devising a method to circulate the paper once it's published."

"But it's free."

"Yeah. The former editors used to just drop piles of the papers in the hallway. This is a class act, not a junkyard. So how do you propose to distribute the *Beam*?"

Eddie paused for a long moment.

Carly was curled under his blanket, with his head on a fluffed pillow. He was really praying that Eddie wasn't scared but was equal to the task.

Eddie stuck his head down over the side rail of the bed, and his unshaved face turned crimson from the pressure of the upside down conference.

"You know the lockers?"

"Yeah, what about 'em?"

"They're those old ones from St. Mary's of the Woods, and they *are* wood. They have those great big vents. Big enough to stuff the paper through."

It was true. Every locker in the halls had great big vents.

Eddie smiled. "Am I hired?"

"Yes, without pay."

Eddie withdrew his head and shifted on his bunk. Carly heard him slap his hands together. He folded up for the night. Carly fell to sleep, too.

After school the next day, Carly spent several hours pushing the refuse out of the way. He accumulated piles in the hallway. The banker's boxes were full and stacked for removal along with 16 black plastic garbage bags.

He started to move some heavy things to the refuse area downstairs. When he lifted the old Ditto machine, he felt a sharp pain in his belly and lost his grip on the 125 pound monster frame. It went crashing to the hallway floor and broke up.

"Uh, oh."

The shattered parts spewed everywhere, including by his feet. Mary Lou was curled up inside the editorial office, under his Lettermen's Club jacket, asleep.

Slowly, sideways, he slipped into the room.

"Lou." His voice whined.

The crash would've awakened a dead cat for another life. He looked at her curled up under the jacket.

When she'd first taken him to the *Chronicle*, she appeared like a Siamese with bright blue eyes, freckled cheeks and a sly smile. He could hardly wait to get that beautiful body in bed.

She stirred, licking her lips, waking up.

"What's the matter?" Her voice sounded alarmed.

"I dropped the Ditto machine." He pressed his hand where he felt the sharp pain.

"Oh my God." She shook her head in denial and pushed up.

She stood in front of him, more than foot shorter, flat in the chest but shaped like a glorious figure eight. She was his perfect match. An array of feelings swept like a brush over his body. She shifted her feet. His breathing picked up. She reached out to him. He breathed deeply. She spoke. He breathed like a horse.

"What do you want me to do?" she said.

His pain went away as quickly as it had attacked. He smiled and wiped his brow.

"Whatever it was, I'm 'kay now, but lifting is definitely over for me. That is something for Big Ed."

"He goes through everything looking for shit. Let's go home."

That was it, he thought. They could do it in her place, under the canopy of her four poster bed, by the pink wallpaper, not on Bareass's tawdry springy bed. She deserved better than that.

He looked around the office that he had cleared. It was about 60' X 60' with no bathroom or darkroom. The floor was stained vinyl tile. Ceiling insulation was marked with water spots. The walls were streaked and smudged. The room had four dirty push-out windows and no shades.

"We've done enough for one day," she said, tugging on his arm.

"Your place or mine?" He grinned.

"Mind yourself."

He looked down. "You're right. I was out of line. But listen, I have an appointment tomorrow to get my release to play ball. I'm not available to work. I need to work out."

"I'll get Melody, Pudge, and Jack to wash the windows and paint the walls."

"What do you mean, Melody, Pudge, and Jack?"

"Do you object to them?"

She was bringing in the losers in the election for her staff. The prospect called for a major objection, down to the mat. He wasn't willing to work with Roos and Mitchem, those irrational people.

"Melody's all right. But I don't want to work with Mitchem. He's crazy. Pudge is tending that way. Her statement to the class suggesting a hot tub and tanning machine if the class elected her editor-in-chief was really loony."

He couldn't tell Mary Lou about the bare-breasted photo.

"You're just jealous," Mary Lou said.

"What do you mean, jealous?"

"I know she slept with your brother at Bareass's. It's no longer a well-guarded secret, Carly Nichols. She's my best friend and *always* will be."

"You've got me," he said, feeling burned by the exposure to her searing tongue.

She took his hand, interpreting "You've got me," to mean that he was freely available to her, rather than Pudge, he thought.

He was freely available to her. Jesus, Mary, Joseph.

"Let's talk about it tomorrow," she said. She pulled his hand toward the steps. Her skin felt moist and delicate like a soft bird.

He stared at her face. It was all right to talk about Pudge and Jack later. He could easily defend his position. She would naturally give up on hiring the losers.

The next morning Carly met with Doctor Szezy. He had to undress, put on a gown and sit on the edge of an examination table. The doctor began by talking about muscle tone and diet. Carly told him about the incident when he lifted and dropped the Ditto machine.

Szezy had him lie on an examining table which was covered with long cloth-like paper. The doctor ran his fingers over the elongated scar from the appendectomy and hesitated a moment. He pressed down slowly.

"Could be a hernia," he said.

Basketball practice started in a week. Carly didn't like Doc's hypothetical tone. The release might not be issued.

"Sounds bad."

"Did you just have that one incident?"

"Yeah. I've been pressing fifty, sixty pounds. Occasionally it'd sting. I didn't think it was anything because it didn't bleed. The pain came and went."

"It's real enough. Sometimes a hernia can get strangulated. That means when your bowel is stuck in a rip of your muscle. The bowel can slip in and out, too. I'll fit you with a strap to hold the muscle closed, but it has to be repaired if you have any hope of playing ball."

Carly was on the floor, down for the count. He turned his head away from the doctor and squeezed his eyes closed with his fingers. His head hurt like it was squashed in a grinder.

He turned back and looked up at the doctor forlornly.

"Don't be sad," Szezy said. "It's done when you're an outpatient. I'll call the surgeon for you." He motioned for Carly to sit up. "You've gained a few pounds. You're up to a hundred forty, which isn't too much for as tall as you are. Your waist is twenty five inches. I'd like to see more improvement on both counts."

He felt panicked. He didn't want to tell Coach Tuttle. Tuttle was counting on him after the two month stint as a newspaper correspondent.

"Will you tell Coach Tuttle?"

"Yes, but you should speak with him, too. He'll have my report on his desk in the morning. Let's see to that strap."

It was so tight in the midriff that Carly could hardly breathe. He had to modify the way he inhaled, concentrating on taking in air higher in his diaphragm, until it became natural. Each breath was measured and distracting. Breathing should be automatic.

Szezy told him to avoid lifting anything more than four pounds. Pressing weights and working out slipped into an indefinite moratorium.

The next morning Carly went to the athletic office. That was located in a wing off the gymnasium, down the hall from the showers, locker and equipment rooms for the boys. It was 11:00 P.M. When Carly walked in and sat on a plastic chair, Coach Tuttle had the report on his desk.

The coach tightened his lips.

"You have a little complication," he said.

Carly looked down at his sneakers. The coach was intimidating.

"Doc thinks I can resume after the procedure." He lifted his shirt and undershirt and curled the fabric so it would remain up.

Tuttle looked at the white straps around his diaphragm, reached and touched them.

"Have trouble breathing?" He picked up the doctor's report. "You'll be out at least six weeks." He showed Carly the report. "I feel like swearing."

Carly took the report, uncurled his undershirt and let it fall over his bony hips.

"Go ahead if it'll make you feel better," Carly said. "Maybe I'll join you." He studied the report and returned it.

"I should be concentrating on how you feel." Tuttle shook his head. "We'll just have to wait. We have to wait for Mark, and we'll wait for you, unless you want to keep statistics."

He had all that valuable experience as an official scorer when he corresponded for the *Chronicle*. The offer was extremely appealing but for his commitment to Mary Lou.

"Take it."

Tuttle raised his bushy eyebrows like his brother, Father Joe, when administering the holy oils.

"You've got to be connected if you have any hope of getting a basketball scholarship to a major Catholic college."

Tuttle drew a measuring tape from his pocket. He stood by his desk, came around to Carly and told him to stand and hold one end on the top of his head. Tuttle hunkered to Carly's sneakers.

"Eighty inches."

"Mark's eighty four." Carly let loose his hold on the plastic tape. It curled down and snapped at Tuttle, who jumped. The tape curled into its case, and Tuttle stood, about even with Carly's shoulders.

"Think where you could go if you were available," he said. "Think where the team could go if both of you were available. Isn't there any chance your dad will be back at work soon?"

"They gave him his release, but then the company laid him off for the winter. Mark is so conscientious that he feels he has to continue at the cleaners. He's 18 now, and he got a scholarship from the company. He's really reluctant."

"But you're not."

"My girlfriend needs me at the *Beam*. Besides, keeping statistics by itself isn't going to get me a free ride. I know I have to play. I have to play all the time and do well."

"I'll think of something," Tuttle said.

16

Mary Lou called a meeting of her appointees and asked Carly to come ten minutes early to make his points about not staffing Pudge Roos and Jack Mitchem. The editorial office was completely furnished. Her rolltop editor-in-chief's desk was located with a view of every corner of the room, the door and steps. The Editorial Office sign was on the door. A large table for planning pages of an issue was against the north wall. New metal files were in place and stuffed with back issues, advertising mats and apples for the teacher.

The windows were draped with curtains to hold off the glare of the afternoon sun. A dozen metal folding chairs were either open or leaning closed against the wall by the door.

Carly came in, grabbed a folded metal chair, slipped it open and sat on it by Mary Lou's rolltop desk.

"Eddie will be along in ten minutes," he said. "I saw Melody downstairs, and she'll be up, too. I don't know about Pudge and Mitch."

Mary Lou was dressed in the school uniform, but she wore his lettermen's jacket. Her pro-life cross, on a silver chain with a key, was prominently over the buttons of her blouse. She looked lovely, but intense about his objections.

"State your case about Pudge and Mitch," she said like hurling a gauntlet.

He told her that Pudge was a dirty girl. When he did, his heart beat faster. He also breathed harder.

Mary Lou detected his physical reaction.

"Have you two been, you know, hitting?"

"No. You know how she is. Remember when she called the Twister Sandwich Shop and asked for a hot dog?"

"I see what you mean." Mary Lou turned away. "She bothers you."

"You should tell her she can't work here. She laid my brother, and she's just out to get a husband."

Mary Lou shook her head and turned back.

"Most of the class is paired off, Carly. I can't just drop her without being accused of discrimination."

"Who's going to accuse the chief?"

"What about Jack Mitchem?"

"I know he put Leon Sweeney up to falling on your party at the skating rink."

"I was never convinced of that."

"I think he's the one behind the saltpeter rumor that almost wrecked the brunch. Suppose he keeps up with his cute tricks and gets arrested? Think how that would reflect on the *Beam*."

"Give me some proof."

The only proof was in his private box at home, the negative from the bare-breasted photo at Pop's place. He couldn't show her that. He'd have to make a general statement. She already knew Mitchem was a goof, yet she wanted him on her staff. The argument Mitchem had made in front of the journalism class in favor of his election was that he'd install a pop machine. Carly leaned forward.

"I wouldn't put it past him to slip something in his stories that was really, really offensive to Father Alexander."

"Like what?" She put her fist under her chin as if she expected a shocking allegation.

"Running *sotto voce* a nude in a sports picture."

"*Sotto voce* refers to the spoken word, Carly. I think you meant to say *subliminal*. Besides, we'd catch it. You'd catch it or I'd fire you."

"'Kay. That's all I have." He sat back in his chair and sighed.

He couldn't convince her. He'd either have to quit and become the statistician for Coach Tuttle or continue to deal with the problems caused by Pudge Roos and Jack Mitchem.

The challenge was staying with the *Beam*. After his initiation into reporting for the *Chronicle*, his momentum was with practicing journalism.

Melody Malone and Eddie Nichols come up the steps.

Eddie stopped by the open door and admired the signage.

"Boy, does that look neat. I think I died and went to hog heaven."

Melody giggled. They grabbed metal chairs by the doorway and pulled up to sit on them next to Carly by Mary Lou's rolltop.

The desk was locked. She turned the little key next to the cross on her chain and rolled up the flexible cover. She took a paper from a cubbyhole on the second shelf and passed it around even though Pudge and Mitchem hadn't shown up. It was her business plan.

She must've talked with her dad about a business plan for running the school paper. It was like her rewriting 15 times the short story before submitting it to a magazine. She was thorough and methodical.

Melody said she just saw Sister Virginia in the journalism classroom. Sister had remarked that the results from the National Catholic Essay Contest would be along in a day or two. Someone from the school had won a prize this year.

Carly looked at Mary Lou. Her stylish story on devotions, he thought, probably had won. He felt happy for her.

He studied the short business plan. It called for doubling the features coverage, sticking with Al the letterpress printer, and adding an insert page for special, rather than institutional, advertising. She projected a profit, which the *Beam* had never turned.

"Advertising comes first," Mary Lou said. "It has a definite lead time. We have just enough days to sell out by New Year's." She looked straight at Eddie. "I heard from Carly your idea for distributing the paper through the locker vents. That's approved. Now, can you sell advertising space?"

Eddie blushed and hesitated like he was scared. "I have a few ideas."

Carly held up his hand. "I'll take him around, starting after my hernia thing tomorrow."

Mary Lou looked surprised. "Is that tomorrow?"

Carly lifted his shirt and T-shirt. He displayed the white bandages around his diaphragm and drew in his breath with a scraping sound.

"It's pretty stifling," he said. "I'm having the operation done."

Mary Lou extended her hand and touched his knee when he dropped the shirts. She turned to Melody.

"He's our first casualty. Dropped the Ditto machine lugging it out to the trash."

"I see," Melody said.

"I want you to do the features," Mary Lou told Melody. "Give me a few of your ideas."

"I thought I'd start with vocations," she said.

Melody wanted to become a nun.

"Work with Carly on that," Mary Lou said.

Melody looked Carly in the face and smiled. They had the double date to the Grotto of Saint Joseph in common, besides his brother, Mark.

"Did you get a cash prize last year?" Carly said.

"Twenty five dollars for tenth place," Melody said.

They all discussed random ideas after Mary Lou's assignments. The excitement of the initial staff meeting died down when it was apparent that Pudge Roos and Jack Mitchem were no shows.

Carly felt relieved. A showdown was deferred. Mary Lou probably knew all the time, passing out the business plan early.

Mom and Dad drove Carly in the F-150 Lariat to St. Francis' Hospital Outpatient Clinic at 7:00 A.M. the next day. Doctor Szezy's surgeon, Dr. Melloy, was going to perform the procedure. His male anesthetist gave Carly a needle about 8:30 P.M. in a cold examination room. Carly woke up after the operation at 10:30 A.M. with a patch bandage covering a wound near his old incision scar. He came out of the anesthetic at noon, and his folks took him home after he was in the hospital 24 hours.

He went directly to bed. The pain from the new wound was sharp. He doubled his medication and drifted off to a dreamless sleep.

The next day his belly hurt deeply and intensely. He felt flattened and slept most of the morning, but at noon Mom woke him up and said he had a phone call.

Mom sorted Christmas gifts for sale at one of her house parties when he came in the living room. He stepped over boxes she'd arranged according to instructions. When he stepped, he winced in pain. Dad was helping Mom sort, and he handed Carly the phone. It was Mary Lou.

"Can you believe it?" she said. "I won a prize in the contest, Carly Nichols." She sounded excited beyond belief.

"How much?"

"Five hundred dollars." She had a great big flute in her voice. "Can you come over to my house?"

"Aren't you calling from school?"

"I took the day off. It's first place. I got a certificate with a gold-embossed seal and a letter of congratulations."

Carly held his hand over the receiver and asked Mom and Dad if he could drive over to Mary Lou's for the afternoon. They looked at each other and nodded.

"See you in a sec," he said.

Suddenly his pain seemed subdued. He dressed without a wince. At the front door on the way out, he dipped his finger in the holy water dispenser and crossed himself. He looked back at his mother, who was smiling.

"Did you take your pain pill?" she said.

"I sure did," he said.

"Have fun," Dad said.

He walked to his Ford, which was parked by the front curb. The weather was chilly. He opened his car door, climbed in and coughed. That really hurt. He felt cold.

He climbed out of the car and held his belly. He decided the pain would go away, but he wanted a cap and coat. He went back inside, collected his coat and cap, came back out, started up his car and drove across town to Mary Lou's house without coughing again.

He noticed a few cars parked in her driveway, indicating she wasn't alone. He went up the winding front walk, past the lawn chairs and catalpa tree, to her front door and rang the bell.

He waited and looked over next door to Pudge's house. More cars were parked in front of Pudge's house than Mary Lou's. Something was up. Relatives must be in town.

Mary Lou opened her door and shouted, "Carly!"

It was an announcement. He was there to aggrandize her victory in the contest. There was a crowd in the hallway with the clock on the wall, mail table and hat tree. He went in cautiously, took off his coat and cap, trying to think of what to say to everyone that would please his wonderful girlfriend.

Dad Reiley was there. So was Mom Reiley, passing out the chips and dip. Melody Malone and the girls from the skating rink bunch that fell onto the slab were circulating in the party mode. They smiled and laughed and asked if Mary Lou wasn't the greatest, exalting her like the queen of the realm.

He thought he was dreaming. He was the only boy. He towered over the girls. He became aroused with the attention, the fawning and the excitement.

Mary Lou came up to him at the hat tree and gave him an envelope.

Carly had written a monotheistic rather than a pantheistic description of the Lord's infusion in nature in America. "Sort of what you would expect from a sixteen-year-old boy," she'd said when she read it.

The envelope had the return address of the National Catholic Essay Contest in the upper left hand corner. Inside was a citation to Karl "Carly" Nichols awarding 100th prize in the category of The Environment and God, but no check.

For one more day he stayed home from school. Eddie brought home his classroom assignment. Tucked between workbooks Eddie had his own admiring card with an inscription: the the best brother in the world, get well.

Beginning to thrive, Eddie had carried on as business manager for the *Beam* by delivering his first work order. At Father Alexander's office, he got the okay for supplies. He'd retrieved the mail from the paper's postal box near Ellie Blan-chard's desk.

Carly planned to take him to solicit advertising as soon as they could walk around town together.

17

He accompanied Eddie on the initial sales calls. The first was Poppachino's Candy Store. Pops bought a quarter of a page for $1,800 at $300 per issue to be paid on publication.

Carly made the sale, because Eddie was too shy at the last moment when he remembered the *EverBloom* book from Tom Bareschitz. Afterward, he dragged along behind Carly on the sidewalk. Eddie was supposed to keep count in a spiral notebook. On the second trip the following day, he forgot the notebook at a call and had to retrace his steps, losing about an hour's selling time.

Carly had to keep the initial accounts, collect the money for Sister Virginia and lay out the advertisements for those who didn't have prepared matrices or mats, as Sister Virginia called them.

In the process of suggesting advertising, Carly and Eddie first met Al, the letterpress printer mentioned in Mary Lou's business plan. He had all kinds of advertising assists. He also had a money-saving proposition about the *Beam* operation.

Al suggested that if St. Basil's switched from letterpress to offset, he could save the *Beam* real money on the printing. No editor prior to Mary Lou Reiley had the desire to change, and her plan didn't either. Al had a reputation for working all night at his Line-O-Type machine to assure a publication deadline. But for the initial issue, Al proposed to eliminate letterpress and use offset.

Mary Lou readily agreed to the offer and had the bright idea of contacting Max Able. He published *The Daily Chronicle*, which was issued using the offset process. She sent Carly and Eddie. Carly thought her dad would probably prepare the publisher for their visit like he did with the donated equipment.

He took Eddie to Able's office, which was adjacent to the editorial bullpen upstairs. They knocked on the publisher's door, and Able himself answered.

He seemed delighted to see the Nichols brothers.

The walls of his large carpeted office were lined with photos of famous people who'd passed through town on their way to somewhere else. One depiction showed where Landers' Landing got its name.

Colonel Landers had established a clearing on the rough bank of the Mississippi River after the end of the Black Hawk War in 1833. The watercolor showed him embarking from a raft holding an American flag in one hand and a musket in the other.

Carly asked Able whether the paper might be interested in further promoting journalism at St. Basil the Great High School by allowing the *Beam* to use the *Chronicle's* offset cylinder-making facilities at a reduced price. Al would make the press run.

"I'll do it for you at cost," Able said.

"Would you like to buy an ad for our paper?" Eddie asked.

Able grinned. "Of course I will. I'll take a quarter page."

"Wow. That's $1,800, $300 on publication of each issue," Eddie said.

Able took Eddie's hand and led him to a door on the east wall, next to the picture window overlooking the editorial bullpen. Able opened the door to his CPA's office.

"Fix up this gentleman with a voucher, will you please?" he said to his accountant.

The accountant looked even older than Able. Slumped over his desk, he wore little half-lens glasses, held an ink pen and worked on a ledger.

Eddie tugged on Able's hand.

"It's on publication, sir," Eddie said.

"I'm sure your issue will come out, young man. We'll start with the first $300 and send you the text for the ad."

The CPA opened a large black checkbook on his desk. He wrote out a business draft payable to St. Basil's *Beam,* signed it, tore it out of the checkbook and gave it to Eddie, who was thrilled.

Carly asked Able for the phone number for the technical director to make arrangements for the offset materials.

"Sounds reasonable," Able said.

Melody assigned Carly to write a story about the vocation of engineering. Dad Nichols called up his boss, Sam Kurwin, for an interview at the Pieper Building Company main office in town. It happened on a Sunday afternoon.

The office was in a complex of buildings near Mary Lou's and Pudge's houses. Carly planned to see Mary Lou after he had his notes. Maybe because it was Sunday afternoon and the heat in the building was turned down, Kurwin's space seemed cold.

Kurwin sat in a big red leather armchair behind an enormous desk, which was piled high with trade publications. The wall behind had certificates, awards and a PE designation hanging in frames. Kurwin chewed gum.

"So you want to be an engineer?" he asked Carly.

"I'm thinking about it."

"Cold or hot?"

"Warm." Carly explained he was writing a story on the profession.

"Outdoor work suits young men." Kurwin smiled. The skin of his cheeks looked rough and red but not from liquor like Ed Newsom. "I remember your dad when he started with us years ago. He's a fine man, your father. I don't even think of him as a laborer."

"Well, he's laid off."

"That's just part of the business. Some years he's not. If he had an education like you're thinking about, why, the salaried men never get laid off. They're planning the next moves. Preparing bids, ordering materials, polishing up credentials and trying to get business."

Kurwin swung around in his chair. The springs squeaked. He slid open a door to a credenza unit against the wall below his citations. He lifted out something and turned back, holding the company's advertising brochure, which Carly had seen at home.

"We distribute that to potential customers. It describes some of the more successful projects in the past few years, like St. Basil's."

"I've heard the term *operating engineers.*"

"They're unionized skilled labor."

"Not real engineers?"

"Not in the sense of a PE." He waved the pamphlet toward his framed professional engineer designation. "Listen, son, whatever you do or write about, it's a great big wonderful world out there, just waiting to be improved. You could put your heart into it and derive the utmost satisfaction." He set the pamphlet down in front of Carly.

Carly picked up the brochure and flipped through the color pages a moment.

"You make useful, practical things."

"Yeah, sure, roads, buildings, sewers. A little bit different from football and basketball."

Carly folded the advertising brochure under his arm and stood. It occurred to him to ask for an institutional ad for the *Beam.*

"Would the firm be interested in an ad in our paper?"

Kurwin, the boss of the company, bought a quarter of a page for $1,800 before he spit out his gum and walked Carly to the door. Kurwin turned around as if he had other work to do in the chilly confines.

Carly went to his car in the nearly empty parking lot. He set the brochure on the bench seat of his car. He realized that the world around him had been shaped by civil engineers.

He wasn't good at math, and he'd always wondered how builders designed bridges, highway interchanges and all those ramps. He'd never really thought about it before, but it seemed that the puzzling and mysterious structures in the world, like the pyramids and Mount Rushmore, amounted to nothing more than gigantic angles, tangents and planes.

He looked up at his driver's side window. Pudge Roos was knocking on the glass. He rolled the window down.

"What are you doing here?" she said. She wore a parka and looked cold but happy to see him.

His heartbeat picked up when he saw her smile.

"I might ask you the same."

He wanted to invite her into the front seat, but it was temptation in spades. He was fighting hard to ward off his feelings for her, but all that work disappeared when he saw her.

Jesus, Mary, Joseph.

"My house isn't too far away, and I was out walking around when I saw your car."

That sounded innocent enough. No fake set-up or teasing routine to make him feel bad. It was an empty parking lot on a Sunday afternoon, for God's sake.

"Hop in," he said. "I was just heading for Lou's after an interview."

When she climbed in the car, his arousal came back in a flash. The resistance built up from his recollection of the tawdry Bareass's rooms, the revelation of her time spent with Mark, his own rejection of her at the staff meeting, didn't amount to a hill of beans. The rush returned. He felt his face flush. He began to sweat. His heart rate picked up dramatically when he imagined her.

"What kind of interview?" she said.

She blinked. Her hair was tied in a ponytail, and it bobbed like her breasts.

"With Sam Kurwin, head of Pieper's."

"Oh, yeah. They gave Mark that scholarship. I'm very happy for him."

Carly paused. "Bareass told me about you and him."

"It was a long time ago."

She put her hand on Carly's leg, just underneath the steering wheel. He placed his hand over hers and moved hers away.

"I was 14, and he was 16, and I think it was his first experience."

"Was it yours?"

"My first was with another boy from school."

"Where did you do it?"

"To tell you the truth, it was at my house. The folks were gone and we just went into my bedroom."

He'd never been in her house, and he didn't know what her bedroom looked like. But he knew what she looked like, and he saw himself playing with her for hours, doing all the exercises in the *EverBloom* picture book several times without regard for safety nets or staying power.

Then he imagined himself with Mary Lou Reiley, when her folks and all the kids were away, going upstairs to her four poster by the pink wallpaper. But the bedroom faded.

He remembered her picking up the phone in his hospital room, looking like a Siamese cat in front of the *Chronicle* Building, lying on her darkly tufted carpet and humming for his kiss. Then she tore up his vandalism complaint form, told him at the picnic table of the Big Ober Root Beer stand she wanted to be editor-in-chief and wrote down the names of all her suitors at the Fall Ball on the little wrist note pad.

Jesus, Mary, Joseph. He still wanted Pudge.

He drove up to the curb by Pudge's house.

She sighed. "I really, really love you, Carly Nichols."

"Why don't you just let me do it at my own pace, like Mary Lou?"

"Mary Lou has her head in the clouds. I can give you what you really, really want. Try me out."

"Like all those extra minutes at Bareass's with my brother?"

"I'd make a good companion. We watched videos."

His stomach rumbled at the thought of Mark watching porn.

"I know you can be warm and comfortable, a companion, if—"

"If what?"

"If you were as smart as Lou, as rich as Lou and as pretty as Lou."

"I can't help it if I developed too early."

"And I can't help it if I can't keep up with all your antics."

She climbed out of the car. She went down the walk to her front door without turning and looking back.

18

Carly drove a 120 yards down the street from Pudge's house and parked by the curb in front of Mary Lou's. He pinched his eyes by squeezing his thumbs and index fingers over the lids. He looked back toward Pudge's.

What a loser. He'd actually had a discussion with her about their relationship. He wondered when she'd take that as a dare and show up at the *Beam* editorial offices and make more trouble. He climbed out of his car.

He went along Mary Lou's winding front walk and stood on the porch. He knocked on the door and heard a voice inviting him in. He opened the door and stood briefly by the jamb. He saw Mrs. Reiley a few yards down the entrance hallway. She pointed upstairs, and he went up the steps to Mary Lou's room.

With her door open, she was sitting on a stool in front of her desk. She wore a white blouse, a short dark skirt, white socks and slipper shoes. She looked dainty and slight. He sat carefully on the soft edge of her four poster bed under the canopy.

"I'm making out my college application. I'm sure I can get into Mount Holyoke. It'll help a lot that I won the national essay contest."

"Do they even accept juniors?"

"They hold the applications indeterminately."

She was really serious about the place. The rules of the admissions game seemed inscrutable to him even with the old girl network.

"What's going to happen to *us*?"

She rotated on her stool and looked directly at him. His heartbeat picked up. She looked concerned. He held his breath self-consciously. She rubbed one of her fingers over a plucked black eyebrow.

"Well, Carly, you're going to college, too. So we'll both be pretty busy."

"You'll be so far way. Aren't you even going to apply in-state?"

"No. Mount Holyoke. My mother would kill me."

"Is she the point person?"

"Look, they have scholarships at nearby schools, Carly. Amherst is ten miles away. Then there's the University of Massachusetts, which has a full service campus with big time sports. Smith for ladies, plus a little school called Hampshire.

They allow you to attend classes at any of the others. I'm hoping you'd get in one of those, except for Smith and Holyoke."

"How much does Holyoke cost?"

"My parents will pay for it. Dad is a millionaire."

Definitely not in my little league, he thought. Mary Lou's scheme of things spread out like a bright line map of the future. He was only a prospective passenger on the shining train.

"Do you think we'll be friends in college?"

"I hope so." She looked determined. "But I don't want to get too serious until I'm finished."

"Which college would you pick for me?"

"The University of Massachusetts, because it's a big campus with all the sports. I think you're happiest when you're on a team." She smiled, but it rapidly diminished.

"Do they have an engineering program there?"

"I think they're mostly liberal arts."

She wanted him to continue with sports. She had the school picked out. But whoever heard of the University of Massachusetts'teams? She'd tossed him a bone. On the surface with her toned down smile it was like a grudging allowance. She could put up with it.

He reached for her hand.

"Am I going to have to wait in the rain for *us* to happen?"

"I don't look at it that way at all, Carly." She took his hand, leaned forward and kissed him on the lip. "Kids don't get married out of high school like they used to. The work place is too complicated. Things are too expensive, especially babies."

"But your dad is rich. He knows I'm your guy."

"I expect my husband to support me, not my dad." She frowned. "Is that what you're expecting?"

He looked away. "I didn't say it right."

She made him an offer. "Let's spend part of my prize money on a dinner out."

"'Kay." He picked up. "Let's go somewhere really nice so I can wear my new suit."

He was trying to fit into her image of a man, and it was a challenge. They'd go to the hotel dining room, enjoy an elegant meal with tenderloins and asparagus. No one would ask about his age. He'd reserve a suite upstairs. Go after dinner. He'd peel off her pretty dress.

"Are you going to make an application to the University of Massachusetts?" she said.

"If you want me to." He nodded vigorously. "It was very thoughtful of you to cater to my need for sports."

"Good." She seemed satisfied. "Let's go to the country club."

"I was thinking of a nice hotel."

"Oh, no you don't, Carly Nichols. I said I didn't want to get serious." She rotated from him on her stool.

He reached again for her hand, touching it, urging her to face him.

She raised her eyebrows.

He softened his voice, hoping that would affect her answer. "I know you're interested."

"I said I didn't want to get too serious, Carly." She looked down. He could tell her resistance was fading fast.

"We'll have a nice dinner with lots of vegetables, like asparagus and drinks made with fruits from Hawaii."

"That's very descriptive."

"We'll look out the window and contemplate the universe and plan our future." He rubbed his hand over hers and put his fingers between hers. He squeezed.

She turned on her stool and looked straight into his eyes.

The fetching Irish virgin was longing for male affection, and he was ready to deliver.

He didn't blink. He felt the beat of his heart rise. His lungs filled with her fragrance. He imagined his hands rolling over her silky smooth breasts, and he wanted to be in bed with her.

It was a different urge than with Pudge, when his whole body demanded satisfaction and he could do it anywhere. It was yearning, more seeking than curious, more wanting than insisting. Just to get close at first would be enough.

They stood by her desk, continuing to hold hands. He felt flushed with the power of his feelings. He wrapped his arms around her head and shoulders, smothering her gently. He pushed his hips toward hers.

"What about your sore stomach?" she said.

"You're not hurting me. You're making me feel better."

"No, no," she said when he ran his hands over her breasts.

He sighed.

He let his arms fall to his side.

She took a deep breath.

"My folks are downstairs," she said, "with Tolly and Molly."

He stood tall, filled with feeling, waiting for her to make up her mind.

"Tolly and Molly," he said.

She yanked his hand and arm toward her open door. He stumbled along. She stopped at the foot of the door.

"Next time we'll meet downstairs."

"Why?"

"Let's just say it's the wrong time of the month."

"What about dinner at the country club?"

"Don't call me, I'll call you." She pushed him out the doorway and closed the door behind herself. She wasn't rough or crude, and he felt it really must be the wrong time.

Pudge showed up at the *Beam* office the next day. He was adjusting the curtains at the window to keep the sunlight off Mary Lou at her rolltop desk. Pudge walked in and looked around.

"I've got news," she said. "Mrs. Johnson just posted her try-out spots for the school play."

Carly went up to her. "How come you found out about it before the *Beam*?" he asked, as if the school newspaper should've had the scoop.

"I've made Pudge the news editor," Mary Lou said, looking at Carly. "She's going to be our snoop."

Pudge walked up to Mary Lou's and sat on a metal chair.

"So what else is new?" Mary Lou asked her.

Mary Lou wore the school uniform, white socks and sneakers. Pudge wore a form fitting dress and black slippers. He thought Pudge had gone home and changed before she showed up at the *Beam*. She looked neat. He went to where the girls sat and pulled up a chair.

"What part are you trying out for?" Carly asked Pudge.

"I'm going for Auntie," Mary Lou interrupted.

"The maid, of course," Pudge said, looking at Carly. "She's the little thing the old banker fucks in the kitchen."

"She does not," Mary Lou said. "The banker falls for Auntie. The maid only *thinks* she's fucking him."

"I better re-read the script," Carly said. "I thought they were both fucking him."

"This is going nowhere," Mary Lou said, turning away.

"Pudge, you'd be the perfect maid," Carly said.

Mary Lou turned back and faced Pudge and Carly.

"By the way, Carly," she said, "whatever happened to your dog?"

"Blackie? Mom takes care of him because she's home all the time. Who takes care of your Whitie?"

"Mom," Mary Lou said, "when she's not at the kennel."

She'd made a gross error in the relative pronoun, and when she realized it she snickered.

Knowing the staid Mrs. Reiley, Carly laughed.

"What's so funny?" Pudge said, not catching on.

The next time Carly went to the weight room to press, Coach Tuttle hailed him and asked him to come into the athletic office. Tuttle looked concerned. He sat behind his small wooden desk, leaned forward and had Carly sit in front. The room smelled like chlorine from the nearby showers.

"I've heard you're applying at the University of Massachusetts at Amherst. Is it true?"

"I promised my girlfriend."

Coach Tuttle showed his displeasure. "That's not a good reason."

"Look, coach, I know U. Mass is nowhere on the basketball map. But, honestly, this hernia thing has me tied up in knots. I may have to settle for something where I can fit in rather than try for something big."

"You're underestimating yourself, boy. You're still growing, and if you stick with it you can be very, very big."

Tuttle's face was taut. He was dead serious.

Carly brightened. A compliment from the coach shaded his views.

The specter of the promise of professional sports reared its head. It was true that he continued to grow, lengthen and stretch despite the muddle in the middle of his belly. The stomach just got softer, bigger. He was starting not to fit into normal areas. His crown pushed up against the header in his car. Some of the machines in the weight room weren't designed for a tall fellow. Sitting in the chair in front of the coach, his head was a good foot and a half above the man.

"Okay," Tuttle said, "I'll give you a recommendation to the college of your choice if you just play at least ten games this season. That would mean you have to be on board by the last of January."

19

Father Alexander called Carly over the loudspeaker to come to the office. It was Tuesday afternoon about 4:00 P.M., Father's regular time to hear students' confessions. He wondered what it was all about when he left the *Beam* editorial room and went straight to the office. Ellie Blanchard told him to go right in. Father was reading from his breviary.

He closed the prayer book, took an unrolled condom from the top of his desk and held it up between his fingers. The nipple of the condom was stuck flat.

"That can't have my name on it," Carly said, waving his arms.

Father didn't think that was funny.

"I got it from Jack Mitchem, or rather from the things in his pocket. He's at juvenile hall."

"What'd he do this time?"

Carly sat on a hard wooden chair in front of Father's sculptured desk. He stared at the beveled sacred hearts and crosses. He had a strange desire to chisel a Cupid's heart and arrow on the wood with the inscription, Carly Loves Mary Lou. But he knew that would never happen.

"Would you mind paying a visit to Jack when he gets home? His folks are at a real estate agents' convention in Las Vegas, and I know he's down and out and needs someone his age to talk with about his problems."

Carly thought a moment. He didn't get along well enough with Mitchem to console him, but Father seemed to think so. Why? Father couldn't know about Mitchem's antics cooking up the saltpeter thing or about the photo from Poppachino's of Pudge's bare breasts, unless he learned about them in the confessional.

"I'm confused," Carly said.

Father smiled. "You've been his pal in the past, and I just thought you might be willing to help him. I'll tell him you're coming to his house. Everything will be clearer then."

Father had learned something in the confessional, but he couldn't exactly say what, because confessions aren't ever supposed to be directly divulged.

Carly nodded. Father came out with a surprising reward.

"I wonder if you'd be willing to serve Mass for me at the Catholic Home start-ing next week through the holidays. Mark helped me out a few summers ago."

"Sure." Carly smiled. "It's an honor."

Father nodded. "We'll have breakfast afterward. I'll see you at 5:30 A.M. at the nursing home chapel next Monday."

When Carly went to Jack Mitchem's back doorway the next night, he used his old-time signal to tell Mitchem he was there, three quick knocks. Mitchem came right to the door.

His pockmarked face, horribly disfigured from bleeding pimples, grimaced when he led Carly inside.

"Beer?" Mitchem said.

"Sure."

Mitchem opened the refrigerator door, grabbed two cans and tossed one at Carly.

"I was pinched, you know. I'm suspended, but they're probably going to throw Sweeney out of school."

They went into the large carpeted living room and sat on sofas facing each other. Between the sofas was a coffee table with a car battery and $15 cash sitting on the top. Carly recognized the battery from his old Ford.

"That's yours," Mitchem said, popping his beer can. The foam ran out on the beige carpet and soaked in.

Carly grabbed the money and stuffed it in his pocket. It's what he'd paid for the photgraph of Pudge with bare breasts.

"I replaced the battery for twelve dollars and fifty cents," Carly said.

Mitchem dug out that money from his pocket and put it on the table.

Carly stuffed that in his pocket, too. He popped his beer can and guzzled it. Mitchem swallowed his beer quickly. Carly drank the rest of his down. They exhaled and belched at the same time, then sat quietly.

"They picked me up for going through houses," Mitchem said.

"I called Father as my nearest relative because the folks have been out of town, and I knew he'd understand my particular bent."

"Bent?"

"Yeah. Did he show you the condom?"

"So?"

"I always put it on when I went into those places. Leon and me never stole much. The action was what we wanted, the excitement of breaking in, moving around in the dark, jacking off and running out into the night with the stolen stuff."

"I see." Carly shook his head. What a loser.

"Mom and Dad want to send me to the military academy in Edwardsville. It's a boarding school." Mitchem's eyes reddened as if he were shaking off tears. "I'm finished at St. Basil the Great High School."

"Is that a fact?"

"I wanted to tell you that you always beat me at everything, and what I did was to show you up."

"No, no." Carly waved a hand. "I never made you do any of those things. I wouldn't even dream half of it. It was your doing."

"When I did it, it was to show you up."

"The battery and the picture I can understand, but not the burglaries."

"You outgrew me."

"Why tell me now when it's too late? We could have had it out in the alley if you had all that much aggression stored up."

"You're a lot taller than me. It wouldn't have been a fair fight." Mitchem paused. "Father Alexander said you'd understand. I told him about the saltpeter thing, the picture of Pudge, the battery, and pushing down Mary Lou, besides the houses we robbed."

"So now you have to go into purgatory."

"Yeah. Military school."

"Maybe that's where you belong."

Mitchem looked like he was hurt. "Is there any way you can talk Father into letting me stay?"

"I thought you said your folks insisted on moving you."

"Yeah, they did. But they'd listen to the priest, too."

"You said you were suspended, which means you can go back after the suspension is over."

"They actually expelled me. I'm history."

"'Kay. Father's having me serve Mass for him at the nursing home over the holidays. I'll bring it up."

Carly looked at Mitchem, who was crying. The tears rolled down his bumpy cheeks like a stream.

Carly felt shaken by Mitchem's confession. He decided he wanted to repeat the visit to the Grotto of St. Joseph in Edwardsville. Mark agreed to take Melody while Carly would ask Mary Lou for her folks' brand new SUV.

Eddie heard about the plans and insisted on going with his girlfriend, Hastie McFarland. Once again an SUV was loaded with freckled Irish lasses and the Nichols boys. It wasn't likely that the new car would break down and keep them from the appointed dates.

The weather was good for late November. The grotto was open on Sunday afternoons. There were no plans for the drive-in movie or root beer stand, which were closed. The plans were for prayer.

Mark brought his book of Psalms, which looked remarkably like Father Alexander's breviary. He started reading from it when they stood in front of the weathered figure of St. Joseph at the grotto.

"I'm going to be a Franciscan brother," Mark said. "Not a priest."

Emboldened by his announcement, he held Melody's hand and expanded his emotions evangelically. He began to sing and rock. He dropped his book of Psalms and raised his hands with Melody toward the clear blue sky. The spirit caught on with Melody. The two wove and rocked to "Onward Christian Soldiers" and "Amazing Grace."

Carly grabbed Mary Lou's hand, which felt cold. He looked at her, and she seemed stultified by the action.

Mark dropped to the ground beside the icon of St. Joseph. He looked struck and breathless.

"A brother?" Mary Lou said.

Carly thought then that Mark had been sleeping with Melody, like he had been with Pudge, for long periods of time behind Bareass's door with the pillow on the floor, but he'd repented. The experience had deepened his love for the Lord.

Melody fell to the ground, and, with Mark, she rolled around in the dead grass, and they moaned like Holy Rollers. The few other worshippers by the grotto were startled.

Mary Lou stared. "It's an act," she said. She looked unmoved. "I wouldn't be surprised if Markie took up a collection when the foam dries up."

On the heels of her opinion, Carly couldn't bring himself to fall down and roll around. But Eddie and Hastie McFarland joined in.

After a moment, Carly felt like he was exposed. The spirit of St. Joseph was beginning to move him. He stood, in transition, over the kids who looked possessed by the Holy Spirit. He too fell down and moaned.

On the way back home, Mark and Melody read Psalms in the back seat behind Eddie and Hastie who ate chips and drank pop.

"Melody is going in the cloister tomorrow," Mark said. "The Sisters of Mercy D'Sanctus Spiritus."

Carly saw Melody through the rear view mirror. She was smiling.

"When did you decide to do that?" Carly said.

"When Mark told me he was going to be a brother rather than a priest."

That must mean they'd lived as brother and sister, avoiding the occasion of sin. Mark's work as a brother would likely involve menial labor rather than liturgical or sacramental work. Carly wished Mark would make a contribution in his own special way rather than laboring in the vineyard of plain hard work.

Mary Lou, in the front seat beside Carly, turned around, agitated, to face Melody.

"What about your job at the *Beam*?" she said. "I knew you wanted to be a nun. That's partly why I picked you to help me, because you wouldn't cause any trouble. But I never thought you wouldn't finish high school."

"They'll educate me at the novitiate for the work I have to do." Melody's face took on the powerful, ghostly appearance of a disembodied spirit. She looked like an angel.

Mary Lou fumed. Carly told her not to worry. The *Beam* hadn't yet even published one issue, and there was time to find a replacement for features.

Then he realized that Pudge could be named the features editor as well as the news editor. She'd likely crawl all over his story about engineers.

"Don't worry about it, Lou," Mark said. "It'll turn out for the better, you'll see. Melody will remember you in her prayers."

Carly looked at Mark in the rear view mirror. He seemed as wan and pale as his girlfriend.

What was he thinking about, quitting high school, leaving behind the possibility of professional sports, and giving up his free ride to Our Lady U. to join the Franciscans?

20

Father Alexander lived on the grounds of The Catholic Nursing Home. It was a red stone conversion formerly owned by a brewer named Eggels, maker of Eggels-brewed Beer. His testamentary devise of 20 acres left the place to the diocese, which contracted for its operation with the Sisters of Mercy D'Sanctus Spiritus. They provided an apartment for Father over a multicar garage, and he provided pastoral services to the community.

The chapel was formerly Eggels' library. Before Mass Carly had the opportunity to browse around and finger some of the gold-edged leather bound volumes of classical poetry, biography and fiction. The room had chairs, not pews. Some of the seats were specially designed for the infirm occupants of the home. Carly felt the solitude of the place. Only three patients were actually present during Mass.

Afterward, Father changed from his vestments into a Roman collar and a black suit. By that time the faint odor of frying bacon wafted into the chapel vestibule. He led Carly through a long, wood-paneled hallway to the back of the home and through the kitchen. Sisters had set a breakfast of bacon, eggs, toast and marmalade in a dining room. It quickly became apparent that Father wanted to talk while he ate.

"I didn't always want to be in the priesthood," he said. "My ambition was to be a chemist. I formulated quite a few new soups in the basement kitchen of my home. Soups are filled with chemical preservatives. My heroes were lab men."

Father surely knew the difference between salt and saltpeter.

"What made you change your goal in life?"

"My sainted mother thought making soup for a living wasn't worthy enough for her boy." He looked drawn and sad, accentuating his bent nose.

Was he sad for his mother, or the incident that bent his nose at one time or for the fact that he dropped chemistry? He couldn't possibly be sad about being a priest of the Roman Catholic Church.

"Turns out there was something to that," Carly said of the maternal advice.

"What hidden agenda do you have, Carly?"

Father dipped a piece of toast into the soft yolk of an egg, bursting the yellow pod into the bread. He chewed the toast and waited for an answer.

"I want to have a family, kids."

That sentiment drew a nod. Father dabbed more toast on the flattened yolk but held the bread while he looked like he was framing his response.

"When's Mark going away to be a Franciscan?"

"When Dad goes back to work and doesn't need his income anymore. When construction season starts."

"I always liked Mark, and he made the right choice. The order pays for everything for the rest of your life." Father chewed on his toast. "It's much better than being a priest for the diocese because of the benefits."

"He's a great guy."

"So what do you want to do besides have a family?"

"My abiding interest is journalism, especially sports writing. I think it's because it was my first big break."

"You mean away from playing games?"

"You can only play ball so long before it gets to you. But you can write forever."

The next morning after Mass, at another huge breakfast, this time including fried potatoes, topics continued to be conversational, but slightly more focused on the school's problems. It seemed obvious that Father was testing Carly for his opinions as an editor of the *Beam*.

Since Father almost never said exactly what he was thinking, there was more to come than a search for his student opinions of matters requiring adult decisions.

"How did you fare with our errant Jack Mitchem?" Father asked.

"I wasn't too surprised." Carly wanted to seem more sophisticated as an editor of the *Beam* than an ordinary jock. "He cried when I talked with him. We used to be very good friends in middle school. He wanted me to ask you to let him back in school."

"That's impossible. It was a decision of the board of directors. I'm sorry. You know, people treat offenses differently these days. Take the environment we live in. Some think that pollution, waste and extravagance are worse than conventional notions of individual responsibility."

"Jack knew what he did was wrong. Up to and including use of the condom you showed me."

"I'm not so sure about that."

"He went to the sacraments, didn't he?"

"Thank God for that. I thank God every day for the Roman Catholic Church, its teachings, its morality and its people. God's grace in the sacraments saves multitudes every day."

Carly was surprised by Father's emphatic statement, which he should've thought was obvious. Father was getting close to his point.

"The diocese has a program for high school graduates that you may not know about, Carly. Subject to qualifications, which I think you meet, the diocese funds your education toward religious life. What do you think of that?"

Carly had to finesse his answer, since Father already knew of his ambitions to get married, have kids and do work in the field of journalism.

"Sounds great. Can I get permission to do an article about that for the *Beam*?"

Carly noticed that Father face, ever-so-perceptibly, looked disappointed.

"I'll see what I can arrange." Father looked trumped. "I was going to speak with Melody Malone when she served Mass, but she's already gone off on her vocation. Wasn't she Mary Lou Reiley's features' editor?"

"Before Pudge Roos." Even mentioning her name, Carly's heart beat faster. A sexual image flashed before his brain, and his breathing picked up. "I have to deal with her now."

"Her dad's the plastic surgeon who advertises on TV, isn't he?"

"He makes a lot of money. They live in a house with a pool, and, and—"

"She lives next door to Mary Lou Reiley."

"I was just going to point that out."

When he finished pressing weights after class, Carly saw Pudge in the editorial office. She'd come in almost every day since her appointment to replace Melody Malone. In an obvious attempt to catch and keep his attention, she first went home and changed clothes out of the uniform. She wore a yellow frock with a ribbon behind her back. Her hair was conservatively straight down. He saw her looking over his draft of the vocational story on engineers.

"This stuff is too dry," she said.

Carly frowned.

Since Pudge had become an editor, she'd displayed a surprising sense of criticism. She had more brains than he formerly thought she had. He had no idea where she dredged up the extra intelligence.

He'd spent hours in the school library elaborating on Sam Kurwin's remarks. He'd brought in electric, industrial, and other designations besides civil. He felt the article was interesting and lucid. But he didn't want to get into an argument, especially now that Pudge had a little power. His own position as assistant to the editor-in-chief was enough to overrule her opinion. Pudge was a minion.

She handed him the red-lined copy. She paused a moment to clasp her hand over his.

Carly looked her straight in the eye. "I'll fix that if you'll let go."

She withdrew her hand.

"Aw, Carly, can't we go somewhere?" She whined. She was almost humiliating herself.

"Not yet. You know, Pudge, one of your faults is that you try to lead people. You have to accept that the man wants to lead you."

She pouted. "You're so old-fashioned. I'd get down on my knees for you. You'd be glad I did."

"You're right." He felt flushed. "But I wouldn't ask for that until the right time, and maybe never."

"Never say never."

"Let's change the subject."

"The try-outs are tonight. Are you going?"

"I have to take my dog."

"See you there." She fluttered out of the room, swinging her arms like she was swimming a race to the doorway.

Carly was lying in bed when he overheard Dad speak with Mark. The topic was the Pieper Scholarship under the circumstances of Mark's expectations to enter the Franciscan Brothers. When the conversation was over, Mark came in the bedroom and plopped down on his bed.

Carly couldn't wait to have the extra space and not have to stare up at the slats under Eddie's bed.

"We have a situation developing about the scholarship," Mark said. He yanked his socks, stripped and put on his pajamas. "Dad wants you to have it when I go." He knelt down to pray. His feet stuck out to the middle of the floor.

Carly didn't interrupt. What a tremendous break for his future education. Mark's bed and ticket in one fell swoop.

When he finished praying, Mark asked if Carly were interested in the scholarship. Carly nodded.

"I asked because I thought you applied to the University of Massachusetts. It's not a Catholic college and doesn't qualify for the funds."

It wasn't a perfect fit, because any Catholic college would be farther away from Mary Lou than the U. of Mass. But Mary Lou's dad had graduated from Boston

College, not too far away. Carly thought that Dad Reiley would be flattered if his prospective son-in-law attended his alma mater.

Boston College had a good reputation. It was the football launching for Doug Flutie of Hail Mary pass fame and maker of the good tasting Flutie Flakes whose profits went to a worthy charity.

"I'd be willing to apply at BC."

Mark lay back and fell to sleep without deciding the matter, but Carly didn't mind. He drifted off dreaming about opportunities, especially with Mary Lou in her pink-papered bedroom.

When he woke up, he looked at Eddie sleeping soundly. He looked at Mark with his feet hanging over the back of his baseboard.

He looked at his watch. It was 5:00 A.M. and time to drive to The Catholic Nursing Home and serve Mass for Father and have a big breakfast and some stimulating conversation.

He said his morning prayers, washed, shaved and dressed in anticipation.

21

He slouched in Mary Lou's chair by the rolltop when Pudge walked in. She wore a skirt and blouse, pretty things, and her hair was bunched behind her head. She smiled at him and said Mrs. Johnson had posted the actors for *The Song of the Dancing Dog.*

"I see you got the part of the old banker," she said.

"Did you get the part of the mistress maid?"

He sat up. His mind filled with a flash of her in his arms.

"Do ya wanna make something of it?" Her face filled with silly anticipation. "Is this the day?"

"No." He stood and walked away from Mary Lou's desk toward the windows.

Mary Lou walked in the open doorway and went directly to her chair. She looked peeved.

"Can you believe it? That stupid Johnson is splitting the casts. She's running them alternatively. I'm only in one."

She kicked her desk.

"Which one?" Carly said.

"That's the bad part, Carly. You're not in mine."

Pudge giggled and waved her hand in Mary Lou's direction.

"He's in mine," she said.

"Well, goddamn it, I'll get her to change that. After all, the play's based on my suggestion. I should have some say on the casting."

"Why don't you let me straighten it out?" Carly said to Mary Lou. "I'll move to your cast, Lou." He went up to her desk and put his hand on her shoulder.

Mary Lou smiled. "Do you think she'd buy that?"

"May be. It's just an innocent shift, like I would have to stand in for your sick partner."

She looked pleased at his tactical planning.

"It's about time for us to go out to dinner."

Carly dressed in his suit. He prepared his Dad's flask to tuck in the breast pocket of the coat. He waited for Mary Lou in front of his house by the curb.

When she drove up at five o'clock, he hopped in and kissed her softly on the cheek. She kissed him on the lips.

She drove into the country south of town. Dinner would be at the Landers' Landing Golf and Country Club, where'd he won the youth golf tournament the previous summer over Jack Mitchem. She chatted along the way about Mabel Johnson, the drama coach, and her repetitive use of the term *dearie*, which was driving Mary Lou nuts. A moment later they parked in the nearly empty club lot.

The clubhouse was mainly designed for the entertainment of its members, from bridge clubs to food service, not for business seminars. The rooms were intimate and full of chairs, sofas and love seats. The dining room was off the bar area.

He wanted to be in the main area by a window overlooking the Mississippi River where barge tows passed by. Mary Lou led him into the bar.

After they sat in comfortable wing chairs, she ordered a glass of wine, but the waiter ID'd her. She settled for a glass of substitute strawberry punch with an umbrella and a slice of orange. He had a frosted glass of root beer. Denial of liquor service annoyed her. She asked the waiter to move them into the main dining room by the window.

He wondered whether her annoyance would stick all night.

"You know, Carly Nichols, I'd do anything for a drink."

She obviously didn't think he'd come prepared. He lifted the flask from the suit coat and poured a drop into her glass. She reached for his hand and tipped it toward the drink and held it there.

"Thank you," she said, smiling. She drank half the contents of the glass in one tip.

What was going on?

"Satisfied?" he asked.

"I heard you're going to BC and not U. of Mass. Is it true?"

"Where'd you hear that?"

"Your little brother, Eddie, our business manager."

"If they transfer the Pieper Scholarship to me, I have to go to a Catholic school."

"BC is more than a hundred miles away from Mount Holyoke."

"They have good sports teams."

"I just think it's terrible you'll be so far away your girlfriend," she said.

"I thought you didn't want to get too serious."

"I don't. But we don't have to get married to have fun. We do have to be close."

He grinned. "I'm for that. Where do you want to go after dinner?"

"Home. The folks took Tolly and Molly out for the night. We'll have the place to ourselves until eight."

The vision of pink wallpaper, the tufted comforter and the lace header of the four poster bed rushed into his brain. It was going to be the night of the big one. She was initiating her own quest for it. Sweet Jesus, thank you!

The waiter set down a gold-edged menu. He noticed that her drink was almost gone, and he asked if she wanted another. She nodded. The waiter went away.

"What would you like to eat?" she asked him.

"I was just going to say the same thing."

"It has to be tenderloin with asparagus."

She was buying into his romantic vision from when she turned him down before. Next they would be lying together and looking at the moon in the universe and planning their future.

"Of course. That's for me, too."

When they left the clubhouse at 6:30 P.M., Carly's flask was empty. He felt he was in control even though his head was swirling. His heart palpitated. His belly had a sweet feeling. His lungs filled with her perfume.

While she drove to her house, he stared at the texture of her cheeks, the length of her arms and the delicate fingers on the steering wheel. Soon those hands would grasp him in love.

She opened the garage door with *Genie*, and they parked. The lights were off, and they kissed. She got out of the car and took his hand.

It was extremely moist. She was dripping in sweat. She was nervous. Would she opt for something funny, like tearing off her clothes and dancing around the house nude in front of the animals? The whole picture could take on new dimensions.

They went into the back entrance. She flipped on the hallway light. He saw the wall clock, mail table and hat tree toward the stairway to the stars. He kissed her, and he ran his hand over her breasts.

It was for real. She didn't push him off. She didn't grab his hand and lead him, stumbling, back to the garage door.

"I love you, Carly Nichols."

"I love you, Lou." He breathed hard.

She led him down the hallway to the door of her dad's den and library. She pushed the door opened and flipped the light switch on the papered wall. She went to a shelf, grabbed a book and sat on the leather couch by her dad's desk.

The book was the *International Book of World Records.*

"We're going to choose something we can achieve together," she said.

"I thought we were going to make love."

"Have you got a rubber?"

"No. Do you take the pill?"

"No."

"Do you keep a calendar?"

"Of course."

"I thought tonight—?"

"I'm not Pudge Roos. Besides," she said, looking at her watch, "we only have an hour before the thundering herd returns."

"But you let me run my hands over you."

"I'm just a little vulnerable, not a lot."

He smiled. "Okay." He touched the book. "What world record can we set together?"

She gave him the book. He thumbed through the pages and noticed plenty of difficult world records, most by young men and women past the age of sixteen. They had talent, stick-to-itiveness and bright ideas.

"Do you think I fit into any of these?" he said.

She took back the book. "I don't know." She flipped through the pages hardly noticing the many achievements listed. She obviously felt flustered.

"Maybe we should wait to set records."

"Yes, let's wait."

"All goods things come to those who—"

"What?"

"Make love."

"Look, Carly, you're the nicest boy I've ever known. You're clean and smart. You look great. But if we do it, everything will change. We have plans. I don't want to spoil them by getting ahead of ourselves."

He could accept that. "But can't we have fun?"

He embraced and kissed her lips. She breathed hard and kissed back. He started to feel aroused.

"Thank you for spending some of your prize money on our dinner. It really told me a lot about how you feel."

"I'm willing to spend more."

"Can we travel somewhere?"

She stood and returned the book to her dad's shelf.

"Let's go into the living and lie down on the floor and play records and watch the Comedy Channel."

She took his hand, which was still moist, and led him to the doorway of the library, out into the hallway. He embraced her, and she tickled his ribs. They ran into the living room laughing.

They heard Whitie barking.

"Where's the dog?"

"In my room. I'll get her." She let go of him and turned for the upstairs.

"I'm coming."

He took her hand and led her upstairs. She followed like a fabric of gossamer, tiptoeing to the top. He stopped in front of the door. Whitie whined.

She opened the door and scooped up the dog, holding her briefly in her arms. She dropped her outside and shut the door with him inside in the dark.

"What's that little red light?" he said.

"The stereo."

"Turn it up."

"I've got a tape of language instruction inserted."

"How about some music?"

"Okay."

It was Yanni, and they danced around the room to his soft offerings until Whitie began scratching on the outside of the door.

"Oh, hell," she said.

"It doesn't bother me."

"My folks will kill me if she scratches the door. They've fixed it twice. It has to be sanded and varnished."

She opened the door and kicked the dog, who went yelping down the hallway. He turned the music down and heard some commotion downstairs. Her folks, brother and sister were back early. It was only seven-thirty.

He felt disappointed.

"I have to go," he said.

"No, you don't."

"Won't they be right up to get the kids ready for bed?"

"Probably."

"You don't care that they'll see us together in your room?"

"No, why should I? They expect me to behave."

That's what she'd done. She'd behaved. He felt disappointed again, but he had made some progress. Didn't everyone accept him as a fixture around the house?

She embraced and kissed him as Tolly raced up the steps. Carly saw that he dressed in a little suit and tie, like a doll.

He passed them while they stood in her doorway.

"Boy, you're tall!"

"Oh, shut up, Tolly," Mary Lou said.

She took Carly's hand and led him downstairs. They ran into her folks in the hallway.

"Did you have a nice time?" her mother said.

"Of course, Mom. We're going into the library."

Her Dad used the hat tree to hang up his outerwear.

"I hear you'll be back on the basketball court by the end of January," he said.

"That's the plan."

"Good luck." He headed for the living room, presumably to feed his coons. Her mom went up the steps to get the kids ready for bed.

Carly went with Mary Lou back to the library. She pushed open the double doors.

"I've thought of a world record we can beat," he said.

"What's that, dear?"

"Not distance, or numbers, or height or weight. Not even a measurement."

"Doesn't it have to be a measurement?"

"I don't think so," he said, plopping down on the leather sofa and reaching for her hand. She sat next to him and cuddled.

"What?" she said.

"It can be an idea."

"What, like things a Nobel prizewinner would invent?"

"Sure."

"Well, what is it?"

"Guess."

"That could take me the rest of my life."

"That's the idea."

"What's so world recordish about that?"

"It's for us."

"Oh, how sweet." She kissed him.

She didn't chide him for being obscure. The fact is, he was beginning to think that he had the heat 16 thing under control. His purient thoughts about Pudge

Roos couldn't compare to the expectations he had for his wonderful new girl-friend and her family.

THE END